KJK PR

VAMPIRES

GRAHAM MASTERTON   KEVIN J. KENNEDY
GREG F. GIFUNE   LEE MOUNTFORD
NICK ROBERTS   RICHARD CHIZMAR
MICHAEL BRAY   SIMON CLARK

Vampires

Vampires © 2023 Kevin J. Kennedy

Edited by Ann Keeran & Kevin J. Kennedy

Cover design by Michael Bray

First Printing, 2023

Other Books by KJK Publishing

Collections
Dark Thoughts
Vampiro and Other Strange Tales of the Macabre
Merry Fuckin' Christmas and Other Yuletide Shit!
The A to Z of Horror

Anthologies
Collected Christmas Horror Shorts
Collected Easter Horror Shorts
Collected Halloween Horror Shorts
Collected Christmas Horror Shorts 2
The Horror Collection: Gold Edition
The Horror Collection: Black Edition
The Horror Collection: Purple Edition
The Horror Collection: White Edition
The Horror Collection: Silver Edition
The Horror Collection: Pink Edition
The Horror Collection: Emerald Edition
The Horror Collection: Pumpkin Edition
The Horror Collection: Yellow Edition
The Horror Collection: Ruby Edition
The Horror Collection: Extreme Edition
The Horror Collection: Nightmare Edition
The Horror Collection: Sapphire Edition
The Horror Collection: The Lost Edition
The Horror Collection: LGBTQIA+ Edition
100 Word Horrors

100 Word Horrors 2
100 Word Horrors 3
100 Word Horrors 4
Carnival of Horror
Inside the Indie Horror World (Non fiction)

Novels and Novellas
Pandemonium by J.C. Michael
You Only Get One Shot by Kevin J. Kennedy & J.C. Michael
Screechers by Kevin J. Kennedy & Christina Bergling
Stitches by Steven Stacy & Kevin J. Kennedy
Halloween Land by Kevin J. Kennedy

Dedication

I'd like to dedicate this book to my beautiful wife, Pamela. I'd also like to dedicate it to my mum, who is one of the most caring people I have ever known, and to my daughter Rachel, who has grown into an amazing woman.

Table of Contents

Laird of Dunain

By

Graham Masterton

"The tailor fell thro' the bed, thimbles an' a'

"The blankets were thin and the sheets they were sma'

"The tailor fell thro' the bed, thimbles an' a'

Out onto the lawns in the first gilded mists of morning came the Laird of Dunain in kilt and sporran and thick oatmeal-coloured sweater, his face pale and bony and aesthetic, his beard red as a burning flame, his hair as wild as a thistle-patch. Archetypal Scotsman; the kind of Scotsman you saw on tins of shortbread or bottles of single malt whisky. Except that he looked so drawn and gaunt. Except that he looked so spiritually hungry. It was the first time that Claire had seen him since her arrival, and she reached over and tapped Duncan's arm with the end of her paintbrush and said, "Look, there he is! Doesn't he look fantastic?" All nine members of the painting class turned to stare at the laird as he fastidiously patrolled the shingle path that ran along the back of Dunain Castle. At first, however, he appeared not to notice them, keeping his hands behind his back and his head aloof, as if he were breathing in the fine summer air, and surveying his lands, and thinking the kind of things that Highland lairds were supposed to think, like how many stags to cull, and how to persuade the Highlands Development Board to provide him with mains electricity.

"I wonder if he'd sit for us?" asked Margot, a rotund frizzy-haired girl from Liverpool. Margot had confessed to Claire that she had taken up painting because the smocks hid her hips.

"We could try asking him," Claire suggested — Claire with her straight dark bob and her serious, well-structured face. Her husband, her former husband, had always said that she looked ' 'like a sensual schoolmistress." Her painting smock and her Alice-band and her moon-round spectacles only heightened the impression.

"He's so romantic," said Margot." "Like Rob Roy. Or Bonnie Prince Charlie."

Duncan sorted through his box of watercolours until he found the half-burned nip-end of a cigarette. He lit it with a plastic lighter with a scratched transfer of a topless girl on it. "The trouble with painting in Scotland," he said, is that everything looks so fucking

10

romantic. You put your heart and your soul into painting Glenmoriston, and you end up with something that looks like a Woolworth's dinner-mat."

"I'd still like him to sit for us," said Margot.

The painting class had arranged their easels on the sloping south lawn of Dunain Castle, just above the stone-walled herb gardens. Beyond the herb gardens the grounds sloped grassy and gentle to the banks of the Caledonian Canal, where it cut its way between the north-eastern end of Loch Ness and the city of Inverness itself, and out to the Moray Firth. All through yesterday, the sailing-ships of the Tall Ships Race had been gliding through the canal, and they had appeared to be sailing surrealistically through fields and hedges, like ships in a dream, or a nightmare.

Mr Morrissey called out, "Pay particular attention to the light; because it's golden and very even just now; but it'll change." Mr Morrissey (bald, round-shouldered, speedy, fussy) was their course-instructor, the man who had greeted them when they first arrived at Dunain Castle, and who had showed them their rooms.

"You'll adore this, Mrs Bright . . . such a view of the garden and who was now conducting their lessons in landscape-painting." In his way, he was very good. He sketched austerely, he painted mono-chromatically. He wouldn't tolerate sentimentality.

"You've not come to Scotland to reproduce The Monarch of the Glen," he had told them, when he had collected them from the station at Inverness. "You're here to paint life, and landscape, in light of unparalleled clarity."

Claire returned to her charcoal-sketching, but she could see (out of the corner of her eye) that the Laird of Dunain was slowly making his way across the lawns. For some reason, she felt excited, and began to sketch more quickly and more erratically. Before she knew it, the Laird was standing only two or three feet away from her, his hands still clasped behind his back. His aura was prickly and electric, almost as if he were already running his thick ginger beard up her inner thighs.

"Well, well," he remarked, at last, in a strong Inverness accent.

"You have all of the makings, I'd say. You're not one of Gordon's usual giglets. "

Claire blushed and found that she couldn't carry on sketching.

Margot giggled.

"Hech," said the Laird, "I wasn't flethering. You're good."

"Not really," said Claire. "I've only been painting for seven months."

The Laird stood closer. Claire could smell tweed and tobacco and heather and something else, something cloying and sweet, which she had never smelled before.

"You're good," he repeated. "You can draw well; and I'll lay money that ye can paint well. Mr Morrissey!"

Mr Morrissey looked up and his face was very white.

"Mr Morrissey, do you have any objection if I fetch this unback'd filly away from the class?"

Mr Morrissey looked dubious. "It's supposed to be landscape, this morning."

"Aye, but a wee bit of portraiture won't harm her now, will it? And I'm dying to have my portrait painted."

Very reluctantly. Mr Morrissey said, "No, I suppose it won't harm."

"That's settled, then," the Laird declared; and immediately began to fold up Claire's easel and tidy up her box of watercolours.

"Just a minute—" said Claire, almost laughing at his impertinence.

The Laird of Dunain stared at her with eyes that were green like emeralds crushed with a pestle-and-mortar. "I'm sorry," he said.

"You don't object, do you?"

Claire couldn't stop herself from smiling. "No," she said. "I don't object."

"Well, then," said the Laird of Dunain, and led the way back to the castle.

"Hmph," said Margot, indignantly.

He posed in a dim upper room with dark oak paneling all around, and a high ceiling. The principal light came from a leaded clerestory window, falling almost like a spotlight. The Laird of Dunain sat on a large iron-bound trunk, his head held high, and managed to remain completely motionless while Claire began to sketch.

"You'll have come here looking for something else, apart from painting and drawing," he said, after a while.

Claire's charcoal-twig was quickly outlining his left shoulder. "Oh, yes?" she said. She couldn't think what he meant.

"You'll have come here looking for peace of mind, won't you, and a way to sort everything out?"

She thought, briefly, of Alan, and of Susan, and of doors slamming.

She thought of walking for miles through Shepherd's Bush, in the pouring April rain.

"That's what art's all about it, isn't it?" she retorted. "Sorting things out."

The Laird of Dunain smiled obliquely. "That's what my father used to say. In fact, my father believed it quite implicitly."

There was something about his tone of voice that stopped Claire from sketching for a moment. Something very serious; something suggestive, as if he were trying to tell her that his words had more than one meaning.

"I shall have to carry on with this tomorrow," she said.

The Laird of Dunain nodded. "That's all right. We have all the time in the world."

The next day, while the rest of the class took a minibus to Fort Augustus to paint the downstepping locks of the Caledonian Canal, Claire sat with the Laird of Dunain in his high gloomy room and started to paint his portrait. She used designer's colours, in preference to oils, because they were quicker; and she sensed that there was something mercurial in the Laird of Dunain which she wouldn't be capable of catching with oils.

"You're a very good sitter," she said, halfway through the morning.

"Don 't you want to take a break? Perhaps I could make some coffee. "

The Laird of Dunain didn't break his rigid pose, even by an inch.

"I'd rather get it finished, if you don't mind."

She carried on painting, squeezing out a half a tube of red. She was finding it difficult to give his face any colour. Normally, for faces, she used little more than a palette of yellow ochre, terra verte, alizarin crimson and

16

cobalt blue. But no matter how much red she mixed into her colours, his face always seemed anemic — almost deathly.

"I'm finding it hard to get your flesh-tones right," she confessed, as the clock in the downstairs hallway struck two.

The Laird of Dunain nodded. "They always said of the Dunains of Dunain that they were a bloodless family. Mind you, I think we proved them wrong at Culloden. That was the day that the Laird of Dunain was caught and cornered by half-a-dozen of the Duke of Cumberland's soldiers, and cut about so bad that he stained a quarter of an acre with his own blood."

"That sounds awful," said Claire, squeezing out more alizarin crimson.

"It was a long time ago," replied the Laird of Dunain. "The sixteenth day of April, 1746. Almost two hundred and fifty years ago; and whose memory can span such a time?"

"You make it sound like yesterday," said Claire, busily mixing.

The Laird of Dunain turned his head away for the very first time that day. "On that day, when he lay bleeding,

17

the laird swore that he would have his revenge on the English for every drop of blood that he had let. He would have it back," he said, "a thousandfold; and then a thousandfold more."

"They never discovered his body, you know, although there were plenty of tales in the glens that it was hurried away by Dunains and Macduffs. That was partly the reason that the Duke of Cumberland pursued the Highlanders with such savagery. He made his own promise that he would never return to England until he had seen for himself the body of Dunain of Dunain and fed it to the dogs."

"Savage times," Claire remarked. She sat back. The laird's face was still appallingly white, even though she had mixed his skin-tones with almost two whole tubes of crimson. She couldn't understand it. She ran her hand back through her hair and said, "I'll have to come back to this tomorrow."

"Of course," said the Laird of Dunain.

On her way to supper, she met Margot in the oak-paneled corridor.

Margot was unexpectedly bustling and fierce. "You didn't come with us yesterday and you didn't come with us today. Today we sketched sheep."

"You've not hurt yourself, have you?" asked the Margot.

'"I've been—" Claire began, inclining her head toward the Laird of Dunain's apartments.

"Oh, yes," said Margot. "I thought as much. We all thought as much." And then she went off, with a wig-wagging bottom.

Claire was amazed. But then she suddenly thought: *she's jealous.*

She 's really jealous.

All the next day while the Laird of Dunain sat composed and motionless in front Of her, Claire struggled with her portrait. She used six tubes of light red and eight tubes of alizarin crimson, and still his face appeared as starkly white as ever.

She began to grow more and more desperate, but she refused to give up. In a strange way that she couldn't really understand, her painting was like a battlefield on which she and the Laird of Dunain were fighting a silent, deadly struggle. Perhaps she was doing nothing more than struggling with Alan, and all of the men who had treated her with such contempt.

Halfway through the afternoon, the light in the clerestory window gradually died, and it began to rain. She could hear the raindrops pattering on the roof and the gutters quietly gurgling.

"Are you sure you can see well enough?" asked the laird.

"I can see," she replied, doggedly squeezing out another glistening fat worm of red gouache.

"You could always give up," he said. His voice sounded almost sly.

"I can see," Claire insisted. "And I'll finish this bloody portrait if it kills me."

She picked up her scalpel to open the cellophane wrapping around another box of designers' colours.

"I'm sorry I'm such an awkward subject," smiled the laird. He sounded as if it quite amused him, to be awkward.

"Art always has to be a challenge," Claire retorted. She was still struggling to open the new box of paints. Without warning, there was a devastating bellow of thunder, so close to the castle roof that Clair felt the rafters shake. Her hand slipped on the box and the scalpel sliced into the top of her finger.

"Owl" she cried, dropping the box and squeezing her finger.

Blood dripped onto the painting, one quick drop after another.

"Is anything wrong?" asked the laird, although he didn't make any attempt to move from his seat on the iron-bound trunk.

Claire winced, watching the blood well up. She was about to tell him that she had cut herself and that she wouldn't be able to continue painting when she saw that her blood had mingled with the wet paint on the laird's face and had suffused it with an unnaturally healthy flush.

"Oh, no," said Claire. She squeezed out more blood and began to mix it with her paintbrush. Gradually the laird's face began to look rosier, and much more alive. "I'm fine, I'm absolutely fine." Thinking to herself: *now I've got you, you sly bastard. Now I'll show you how well I can paint. I'll catch you here for ever and ever, the way that I saw you; the way that I want you to be.*

The laird held his pose and said nothing, but watched her with a curious expression of satisfaction and contentedness, like a man who has tasted a particularly fine wine.

That night, in her room overlooking the grounds, Claire dreamed of men in ragged cloaks and feathered bonnets; men with gaunt faces and hollow eyes. She dreamed of smoke and blood and screaming.

She heard a sharp, aggressive rattle of drums — drums that pursued her through one dream and into another.

When she woke up, it was still only five o'clock in the morning, and raining, and the window-catch was rattling and rattling in time to the drums in her dreams.

She dressed in jeans and a blue plaid blouse, and then she quiet-footedly climbed the stairs to the room where she was painting the laird's portrait. Somehow, she knew what she was going to find, but she was still shocked.

The portrait was as white-faced as it had been before she had mixed the paint with her own blood. Whiter, if anything. His whole expression seemed to have changed, too, to a glare of silent emaciated fury.

Claire stared at the portrait in horror and fascination. Then, slowly, she sat down, and opened up her paintbox, and began to mix a flesh tone. Flake white, red and yellow ochre. When it was ready, she picked up her scalpel, and held her wrist over her palette. She hesitated for only a moment. The Laird of Dunain was glaring at her too angrily; too resentfully. She wasn't going to let a man like him get the better of her.

She slit her wrist in a long diagonal, and blood instantly pumped from her artery onto the palette, almost drowning the watercolours in rich and sticky red.

When the palette was flooded with blood, she bound her paint-rag around her wrist as tightly as she could and gripped it with her teeth while she knotted it. Trembling, breathless, she began to mix blood and gouache, and then she began to paint.

She worked with her brush for almost an hour, but as fast as she applied the mixture of blood and paint, the faster it seemed to drain from the laird's chalk-white face.

At last — almost hysterical with frustration — she sat back and dropped her brush. The laird stared back at her — mocking, accusing, belittling her talent and her womanhood. Just like Alan. Just like every other man. You gave them everything and they still treated you with complete contempt.

But not this time. Not this time. She stood up, and unbuttoned her blouse, so that she confronted the portrait of the Laird of Dunain bare-breasted. Then she picked up her scalpel in her fist, so that the point pricked the plump pale flesh just below her navel.

"The sleepy bit lassie, she dreaded nae ill; the weather was cauld and the lassie lay still. She thought that the tailor could do her no ill."

She cut into her stomach. Her hand was shaking but she was calm and deliberate. She cut through skin and layers of white fat and deeper still, until her intestines exhaled a deep sweet breath. She was disappointed by the lack of blood. She had imagined that she would bleed like a pig. Instead, her wound simply glistened, and yellowish fluid flowed.

"There's somebody weary uh' lying her lane. there's some that are dowie, I trow wad be fain . . . to see that bit tailor come skippin' again."

Claire sliced upward, right up to her breastbone, and the scalpel was so sharp that it became lodged in her rib. She tugged it out, and the tugging sensation was worse than the pain. She wanted the blood, but she hadn't thought that it would hurt so much. The pain was as devastating as the thunderclap had been, overwhelming. She thought about screaming but she wasn't sure that it would do any good; and she had forgotten how.

With bloodied hands she reached inside her sliced-open stomach and grasped all the hot slippery heavy things she found there. She heaved them out, all over her painting of the Laird of Dunain, and wiped them around, and wiped them around, until the art-board was smothered in blood, and the portrait of the laird was almost completely obscured.

Then she pitched sideways, knocking her head against the oak-boarded floor. The light from the clerestory window brightened and faded, brightened and faded, and then faded away forever.

They took her to the Riverside Medical Centre but she was already dead. Massive trauma, loss of blood. Duncan stood in the car-park furiously smoking a cigarette and clutching himself. Margot sat on the leatherette seats in the waiting-room and wept.

They drove back to Dunain Castle. The laird was standing on the back lawn, watching the light play across the valley.

"She's dead, then?" he said, as Margot came marching up to him.

"A gruesome thing, no doubt about it."

Margot didn't know what to say to him. She could only stand in front of him and quake with anger. He seemed so self-satisfied, so calm, so pleased; his eyes green like emeralds, but flecked with red.

"Look," said the Laird of Dunain, pointing up to the birds that were circling overhead. "The hoodie-craws. They always know when there's a death."

Margot stormed up to the room where — only two hours ago — she had found Claire dying. It was bright as a church. And there on its board was the portrait of the Laird of Dunain, shining and clean, without a single smear of blood on it. The smiling, triumphant, rosy-cheeked Laird of Dunain.

"Self-opinionated chauvinistic sod," she said, and she seized the art-board and ripped it in half, top to bottom. Out of temper. Out of enraged feminism. But, more than anything else, out of jealousy.

Why had she never met a man that she would kill herself for?

Out in the garden, on the sloping lawns, the painting class heard a scream. It was a scream so echoing and terrible that they could scarcely believe that it had been uttered by one man.

In front of their eyes, the Laird of Dunain literally burst apart. His face exploded, his jawbone dropped out, his chest came bursting through his sweater in a crush of ribs and a bucketful of blood. There was so much blood that it sprayed up the walls of Dunain Castle and ran down the windows.

They sat, open-mouthed, their paintbrushes poised, while he dropped onto the gravel path, and twitched, and lay still, while blood ran down everywhere, and the hoodie-craws circled and cried and cried again, because they always knew when there was a death.

Gie me the groat again, canny young man; the day it is short and the night it is lang the dearest siller that ever I wan.

"The tailor fell thro' the lyd, thimbles an ' a'. "

The End

Vampyrrhic Pay-Per-View

By

Simon Clark

"If something has four legs, a tail and barks, it's a dog, right? If something spends the hours of daylight in a grave and consumes blood, then surely we're talking **VAMPIRE***... aren't we?"*

We sat in front of the computer screen. The male voice spoke in that deep, resonant manner redolent of TV commercials for beer. Onscreen, a photograph of a cliché female vampire: a beautiful woman, raven black hair cascading down over an artfully torn dress that revealed just enough bare skin to get my friend sweaty and excited. All of this, however, scared me.

"Murray," I said. "Why do you want to talk to a vampire?"

"Can you think of anything better to do?"

Photographs of the beautiful woman flowed across the screen.

"Look at what they've done to her, Murray. Someone locked her into a cell."

"What do you expect? She's a vampire. If she isn't locked up, she'll attack people in the studio."

The iron bars that formed the cell had been bolted to slimy brickwork.

"That's no TV studio," I told him. "That's some stinking basement."

"Shush... have another." He handed me a bottle. "We're next."

"Murray. Let's take these beers outside."

"This will be amazing. I actually get to meet a vampire online."

"It's got to be fake. She'll be an actress... I hope to God she is an actress, because what they're doing to her is illegal."

A male voice rumbled from the computer. *"Enter your credit card details now. Then select how long you want to talk to Carenza. $100 buys ten minutes. $150 buys twenty."*

"Damn it, Murray." The beer went the wrong way down my throat. I choked out a heck of a lot of beer froth with the words: *"$100!* They're ripping you off. This is fake – mega fake!"

"This isn't fake." The voice came from the PC (not Murray who busily typed his house number and street name into the billing address box).

I stared at the screen as a man's face filled it. His shaved head gleamed. He had the mean eyes of one of those guys who hurt people for a living. A real leg-breaker for hire vibe.

"He can see us." Murray sounded excited. "Look, our webcam's on. He sees us! We see him!"

I rolled my chair back. Okay, maybe I'd drank so many beers my brain wasn't working like it should, but I really believed the hoodlum could reach out of the PC and grab me by the throat.

"Do it!" Murray sang out. "Show me the vampire!"

"One moment, sir. I'm waiting for your credit card to go through." The man's mobster face was replaced by a rotating egg-timer.

I whispered to Murray, "Don't go any further with this."

"I've paid my $100."

"Please, Murray. It's not right; you're going to end in all kinds of trouble."

The hoodlum reappeared onscreen. "Payment accepted. Thank you, sir. Now I'll introduce you to Carenza. Queen of the Vampires."

The man we saw via the webcam moved to one side. We both gasped when we saw what was in the background. The beautiful woman, with the luscious black hair, stood behind the bars of that evil-looking cell. What we saw must have been filmed using something like a phone or tablet, because the image wobbled as the guy picked up the device and carried it toward the cage. This gave the impression of Carenza's face zooming into close-up behind the bars. The prisoner's eyes were a striking almond shape and black as night-time. She wasn't frightened. She wore a neutral expression, neither welcoming nor hostile. Perhaps she'd resigned herself to being confined to that dreary basement with the wet walls.

Mobster-man spoke off-camera. *"Say hello to your guests, Carenza."*

"Good evening, gentlemen." Her voice purred with sultry eroticism.

"Murray, you're being conned!" I wailed. "She's not a real vampire. It's all fake."

The online mobster snarled, *"You want proof? I'll show you proof."*

I can still vividly recall every detail of the shocking scene that followed **(put your hands over your ears for the next few seconds if you don't like descriptions that are too gruesome… and downright nasty).** He continued to film the woman in her cell. As he did so, he opened a window blind high up on the wall (it must have been one of those basement windows set just above ground level). The setting sun fired a beam of light into the basement. The mobster told us to keep watching, and get our money's worth, "because *Vampyrrhic Pay-Per-View* never issue refunds." He ordered the woman to stand in the daylight. A vertical strip of red sunlight fell onto her upraised face. I couldn't stop myself from yelling in horror at what I saw next. Where the red glow of sunset touched one side of her face, a vertical line of skin, corresponding where the light fell, instantly puckered. Skin bubbled, shrivelled, and shrank. It was like watching a plastic mask burn. Carenza threw back her head, arched her back, and screamed.

31

"There's your proof, gents. Natural daylight is death to a vampire. Okay, that's enough." He closed the blind. Within seconds, the skin healed itself. The woman's face was unmarked and stunningly beautiful once more. *"Okay, what's the first question you want to ask her?"*

What we'd seen had shocked us so much we just sat there, saying nothing.

"Get your hundred bucks' worth, guys." He smirked. *"After all, for the next ten minutes she's all yours."*

Murray couldn't speak, so I asked, "Carenza? You really are a vampire?"

In that sexy whisper she said, *"Yes."*

"And you're Queen of the Vampires?"

"Are these banal questions the ones you really want to ask?"

Murray gulped his beer in one huge, terrified swallow. Man, he really needed that alcohol. This was his tenth beer of the night – he swayed as he stared at the tempting, voluptuous figure onscreen. Tempting for him, that is. I wanted out of Murray's basement. Talking to a caged vampire froze my blood. I admit it, I was scared.

Off-camera, Mobster man said, *"Nine minutes left."*

I asked, "You really do drink human blood?"

"For goodness' sake." Carenza lost patience. *"I'm a vampire. Yes, I drink blood."* Her tongue caressed

her lips. *"Won't your handsome friend ask me an intelligent question?"*

Murray blinked. "Me? You want me to ask you something?"

"I'm looking at you, aren't I?"

"Carenza?"

"Yes?" She purred with sexual intensity. *"Ask me anything your heart desires."*

"How long have you been a prisoner?"

"Who said anything about me being a prisoner?" She curled her fingers around one of the vertical iron bars. *"Haven't you noticed? The lock is on my side of the cage. And I have the key."* She touched a key that hung from a red leather belt that tightly cinched her waist. *"I'm not the prisoner here. I'm free to roam."*

"Eight minutes left."

So, Mobster man is the captive, not the other way round, I told myself. *A mortal slave to the vampire queen, no doubt.*

"Please," she murmured with a come-hither look into the camera, *"ask questions that excite me. Be inventive. Take me by surprise."*

"Okay, I will!" Murray suddenly became animated. **"SHOW ME YOUR WORLD!"**

The woman moaned with pleasure. *"Ohhh… now that is a lovely question. The best ever."* She smiled warmly. *"Follow me, boys."*

33

Shivers poured through me. "How can we follow? We're watching you on a computer."

"Where there's a will there's a way." She extended her hand from between the bars. *"Give me the phone."* Mobster-man obeyed. We saw the picture tilt and turn as she took the device. *"Now, come with me… I'll show you my secret realm."* Her red lips formed a delicious smile. *"It's the world below your world."*

She carried the phone, and we watched what she captured for us. We saw it all live as images streamed from the device to the computer in Murray's basement.

And this is what we saw: -

Brickwork – dull and wet. A glimpse of Mobster man beyond the bars – prisoner of the vampire queen. Suddenly, in front of us, an iron door. Her slender fingers pushed it open. The camera seemed to float through the air as if it were a spirit.

"Darling boys, you asked to see my world." There was pleasant laughter in her voice. *"And so you shall."*

I tugged Murray's arm so hard that beer spilt from the bottle onto his lap. He never even noticed – the temptress enchanted him.

"Murrray," I whispered. "Don't watch anymore."

"We're seeing things no human being has ever seen."

"We're seeing things that no human being is MEANT to see. This is forbidden, blasphemous stuff."

"I want to see where she takes us."

"Pull the plug. We could go to a bar instead. Meet girls – living, warm-blooded girls."

"Not scared, are you boys?"

"Not me, Carenza!" Murray sounded eager to please.

"Tell your jittery friend he will see marvellous things tonight. Sexy, exciting things."

This made me reconsider exiting the basement. "Sexy, exciting things?"

"Just follow Carenza." She turned the phone to reveal her friendly, smiling face. *"Keep watching... this is my world."*

The phone's camera revealed a pool of shadow. Moments later, that gloomy void opened out into a huge cavern. There seemed to be no end to the place. Its smooth walls were carved from bedrock, and... *oh!* ... people. Thousands of people. As Carenza walked, they turned and bowed to their queen. Then they went about their work.

"They're miners." I gasped. "Look! Picks, shovels, drills, trucks!"

Sometimes we glimpsed faces in close-up. They possessed inhuman, glittering eyes; lips parted revealing sharp, vampiric teeth.

I stared in amazement. "Bloodsuckers! A race of blood-sucking vampires living underground."

35

Carenza explained: *"We've been hunted by your kind for centuries. Therefore, we decided to create a world beneath the surface. It's always dark here. And our enemies can't find us. At last, we're safe."*

I pictured Carenza, queen of the subterranean vampires, walking regally through the never-ending cavern, her long, black hair swishing as she proudly tossed her head. She held the phone in front of her, at the height of that noble chin of hers. We saw from her point-of- view. Trucks clattered along railroad tracks. They were full of male and female vampires. I glimpsed tunnelling gear: heaps of picks, hammers, sacks of cement – everything those creatures required to build their underground city, their necropolis, their realm of the undead.

For the first time, I asked an intelligent question, "Carenza, if you've got all this construction going on, why do you need Murray's one hundred bucks?"

"My darling boy, all this costs money. We have mortal intermediaries who buy construction materials from builders' merchants on the surface."

I gawped at a dozen bulldozers chugging along a subterranean highway. "It must cost millions."

Murray nodded. "The hundred dollars I paid wouldn't even cover the cost of filling up the tank of just one of those bulldozers."

"You are perfectly correct, Murray. Then I'm sure you're perfect in other ways, too."

He blushed with delight.

"Considering that we're building catacombs that extend beneath the Atlantic all the way from America to Europe, then our need for liquid cash is as insatiable as our appetite for blood."

I whistled. "You're going to have to spend an awful lot of time entertaining pay-per-view clients."

Steps appeared in front of Carenza. We watched from Carenza's point-of-view as she climbed the staircase, which rose up through a shaft in the roof of the cavern. I checked the time onscreen.

"Hey, Carenza? What's happening?" I felt cheated. "There's one minute left on the pay-per-view clock. You promised to show us something sexy."

"I did, didn't I, boys?"

"So…" Murray licked his lips. "When are you going to deliver the goodies?" He eyed the enticing lines her shadow cast on the wall.

I whispered in his ear, "Don't get any weird ideas about Carenza becoming your girlfriend."

He elbowed me in the chest. "Shut up."

I realized what Carenza was doing. She'd hooked two boozy fools (us!) with salacious promises of vampiric erotica – now she'd demand we buy more pay-per-view time. "This is a rip-off," I said. "We're not going to waste any more money on seeing stupid caves."

"Don't worry, boys. Carenza always keeps her promises. You wanted to see sexy, so I'll show you sexy."

She reached a metal trap door set in the cave's roof, which was just inches above her head (or so I judged from the camera angle).

I was getting all argumentative. "And I still don't see how you appearing on a webcam for $100 a time's going to pay for Vampire Grand Central down there."

"Boys, my darling boys, you don't think I'm the sole performer on Vampyrrhic Pay-Per-View? There are thousands of us providing online entertainment."

Murray was drunk. No doubt about it. Drunk as a skunk on payday. "Hey… a promise is a promise. You said you'd show us something sexy."

"And I'll keep that promise. Trust me, you're not going to believe your eyes." She held the phone at arm's length. This way the vampire could film herself standing just inches beneath the steel trap door. *"Okay. Get ready. You're just about to see me **in the flesh**."*

I snorted with disbelief. "How you going to do that? We're watching you on the computer. You're nowhere near this…" My voice died the moment she knocked on the metal trap door.

"Here I come, boys."

I turned down the volume on the computer's speakers. She knocked again.

We both heard that tap of her knuckles against the trap door. The sound came from the steel slab set into the floor of Murray's basement.

"Oh, God," I groaned. "Oh my, dear God."

"Carenza's coming up, boys. You're going to see her in the flesh." The sound of her voice came from beneath our feet.

Onscreen, the vampire queen pushed open the trap door. In Murray's basement, the steel slab began to rise. I could see through the gap. And there, gazing back at us, were a pair of beautiful, almond-shaped eyes.

*

That's it. I've told you the story of what happened to Murray and me. What's that? You want to hear what happened next? You want to know what Carenza did when she climbed up into our basement?

Of course, I can tell you. I can reveal events of such intensity they will shock you. But your time is up. Please enter your credit card details again. A further ten minutes costs only $50.

Oh, and be sure to carefully enter your billing address. That's the full address with house number and street name. Here at *Vampyrrhic Pay-Per-View* we value your custom. And we'd love to keep you with us – late into the witching hour.

The End

The Nest

By

Kevin J. Kennedy

Forks of lightning tore the sky apart. The heavens had opened hours earlier and the team had been well and truly soaked through before they arrived at their destination. The dilapidated mansion lay before them. Each of the team lay in the dirt, not moving a muscle. Neither the ice like rain nor the task ahead would affect the five souls that lay in the mud. Each had their own reason to be there.

None of them has spoken to each other much, but none the less, they were bonded like brothers. Each of them had a matching goal. To eradicate the vermin that had taken their loved ones. It mattered not whether each had lost a husband or wife, child, or parent. None of them had ever asked the others for details. It wasn't relevant. They had a common enemy, a common hatred, a common goal. Each of them would die at the hands of the monsters that took their family, but not as victims. As a bringer of death. If they were taken down, they would die a warrior's death. Not for the pride of it, but because they had nothing left to live for. None of them wanted to be remembered. They all wanted to die, but not before they sent as many monsters to hell as possible.

Each man knew that they would fight until there was no fight left in them, and right now, they lay across the road from one of the largest dens they had ever discovered.

The five men had been scoping it out for the last forty-eight hours. They had seen some of the lesser demons come and go the evening before, but they knew not whether there were any more powerful older beings inside. Four of them were accustomed to waiting and watching but the new kid was twitchy. Eager to get going. It was typical. At the start, they all just saw revenge. The rage was too much, and it drove them, but with haste, mistakes were made. The young buck knew better that to move without being told to do so.

The team of four had found him weeks earlier. He was a solo hunter. They never lasted long as vamps tended to stay in packs. Most of those who went after the vamps on their own ended up in a nest before too long and were torn apart before they could stake their first vamp. Lucky for the kid the team came along to eradicate the nest that the youth had chosen. They let him come in behind them and he killed a few of the vampires that moved on all fours. Everyone in that nest had been lower-level vampires but the youngster would still have died had they let him go in alone.

After the nest was extinguished and set alight, they took the kid back to base with them. No one asked him his name. They left their old lives behind when they became hunters. They called him Newby simply because he was new. The others had been hunting for years together by that point.

No-One was their leader, for no other reason than he was the first. The rest had been the rare solo hunters that had been lucky enough to be found quickly by him, before they perished. Each of them had joined with No-one at different times, but he had been doing it the longest and when the second joined the group, No-One was the more experienced of the two so naturally took a lead role. None of them had ever questioned it. He knew how to plan, was good in a scrape and was always loyal to his team. He had saved most of their asses more than once.

Giant was the first person to join No-One. They travelled together at first with no real plan other than to seek out nests and kill everything inside. Giant stood at just under seven foot tall and had a bulk to match his height. When they weren't hunting, he was eating or lifting weights. Natural genetics from his Swedish heritage played a large part. It was impossible to look at the guy without knowing he was descended from Vikings.

Psycho came next. When they came upon Psycho, he was fighting three young, bipedal vampires at once. While not the smartest of creatures, they were fast and strong. No-One and Giant stood back as he danced round about them and taunted them like a boxer who knew he had his opponent beat. The vampires weren't aware enough of human ways to know they were being taunted. They just continued to swipe and dive for him. He was doing it purely to amuse himself. Young vamps were more animal than human. It was only their body shape and stance that likened them to people. Psycho, on the other hand, struggled to appear human most of the time. His entire body was a mess of scars. Some from vampire battles and some self-inflicted. He always told the others that pain helped. None of them enjoyed the hunt more than Psycho. Although he was crazy, he never put the others at risk, and he was always first into dangerous situations taking the biggest risks upon himself.

The last to join the group before they found Newby was Words. They called him Words because he didn't speak. A vampire elder, after draining Words' wife and two children, had torn Words' tongue from his mouth. He was left for dead but somehow hung on. Paramedics saved his life, but he wished they hadn't. His face was a mask of pain from that moment forth. He was stoic in nature, and they often found him lost in thought. The only time he came alive was in battle. The four of them made a solid unit. They had never lost anyone since coming together and now there was five.

Each of the older hunters knew they would need to keep an eye on Newby, but they had each taught him a lot leading up to this night. The thunder and lightning were getting worse and the rain heavier.

The house was quiet. Most of the windows were boarded up. The doors were boarded too but from where they lay, they could see the back door had been kicked in. They knew that was the only visible point of entry but had no idea if the vampires had created any other routes in or out that they couldn't see. No-One signalled to his team, and they began moving forward. They kept low, knowing the lightning would give away their arrival should they be seen from the holes between the boards.

They were almost at the door when two of the dog-like vampires came shooting out. At first the team thought they had been seen and expected every vamp in the house to come charging out, but it was just the two of them, heading out for the night's hunt. Psycho was first to move as always. He kept himself in good shape, apart from the cutting, but he liked the pain of training hard too so was rarely one to rest. An active, haunted mind was a hard thing to quiet. He was sprinting across the ground between the vamps and the team while the others were still making sure no other vamps were following the first two. Pyscho drew the two crossed swords from their sheaths on his back and beheaded the two blood suckers simultaneously. They had only begun to turn in his direction as they smelled him before he sliced through their necks. An older vamp would have never made such a mistake, but the hunger tore at the younger and lower-level vampires so intensely that they were too focused on feeding.

There were no instruction manuals on vampires. It wasn't like the movies. The team had some knowledge that they had learned through time, and they had a few educated theories, but they still learned new things from time to time. The reality is, none of them had expected to survive as long as they had when they began hunting vampires. It had been a means to an end that didn't feel like a cop out. They were driven purely by revenge but as the numbers that each of them dispatched grew, they had become more serious and organised.

Psycho gave a casual wave to the others and dove back to the ground, starting to crawl towards the door as the others rushed to catch up. He always had to be first.

When No-one and the others got to the door Psycho had gone ahead. No-one drew his sword while Giant brought his double-headed axe around in front of him. Words carried two hunting daggers that he had drawn as he got to his feet, and the kid, Newby, was holding the same two guns they found him with. They were loaded with iron bullets. Iron was fatal to the vamps and a shot to the head would kill them instantly. They slipped through the door one at a time into the darkness.

Inside the mansion was quiet. It was warm and muggy, even though the rain was torrential outside. Dust mites floated in the air, caught in a dance in the little amount of light coming in through the broken boarded windows. Most of the wooden slats crossing the windows were broken as well now, allowing the moonlight through, and when the lightening flashed, it lit up the whole room. They had come in through the kitchen. It was a large room, and they found it as dilapidated as they expected. It had clearly been an age since anyone lived there before the vamps moved in. No-one led the way, through the room and stopped at the first door. Psycho was gone and the door still stood shut, meaning he had likely gone ahead into the house on his own. The large door in the middle of the room was wedged shut but Giant leant in and pulled it open with one hand. Stairs led downward.

The four members of the team that was left in the kitchen started down the stairs. The basement was darker as there were no windows. The odours coming up from it let the team know that there was either vampires down there or several dead bodies. The stairs turned to the left near the bottom, leaving a further four after the turn. As No-one hit the fourth stair up, he stopped and raised his sword. Giant stepped down onto the stair next to him, almost knocking him over with his bulk. Across the room, towards the back corner there were several vampires bent over and feeding on what looked like a young woman. All No-one and Giant could see was long blonde hair hanging off the table that her body was on but everything else was blocked by the vampires that fed on her. They looked withered but not by age. They were recently turned and had a lot of feeding to do. There were six of them noisily slobbering away. The hunters heard sounds of flesh tearing as one of them ripped a chunk from the woman. The newer vampires always consumed flesh as well as drinking blood. As No-one and Giant stepped into the basement, a few of the vampires turned while a few others continued feasting.

A few seconds passed then four of the vampires started moving towards the new blood that had entered their domain. It was instinctual that they would try to drain anyone that crossed their paths. Self-control wouldn't come for some time. One of the vamps pounced at No-one but it was Giants' axe that cut the vampire in half as he stepped around No-one and swung it in an arch. As the two parts of the body crashed to the ground, the legs lay still but the beast began dragging its upper body toward them. No-one swung his sword and decapitated the second vampire of the group while Words stepped forward and put a bolt from his crossbow through the crawling vampire's head.

The vampires that had stayed feasting on the blonde woman had now joined their brethren. The four of them spread out as the hunters did the same. The men were ready for action and the vampires were ready to eat. Newby was the first to move. Maybe it was nerves or maybe he was raring to get going but

47

he drew both his guns and blew the head clean off the vampire that was standing in front of him. A split second later, Giant had buried his double headed axe in the skull of his vampire. No-One and Words had removed the heads of the next two vampires the second after. It was precision work and it had gone like clockwork, but they all knew that these types of vampires were nothing compared to what they may face.

Words turned first and started to make his way back up the stairs when there was a crash from above. Parts of the ceiling started to rain down on the others as they jumped back. The four of them looked up as plaster and wood burst inwards and covered the dead vampires. One by one three older vampires dropped into the room. They looked mostly human. That was the easiest way to tell when a vampire matured. They no longer looked like the walking dead. Their skin colour was off, but you couldn't really notice in low light. That and the fact that there were mouthfuls of fangs jaggedly sticking out of their mouths. The fangs could be retracted so it wasn't always a way to spot older vamps but when they were ready to battle, their fangs were always out. The older vamps sometimes grew additional sets of teeth, much like sharks. The older they got, the more terrifying their fangs became.

The four hunters stepped back into the basement room from the stairs. It was extremely unusual to find three older vampires together.

Sometimes two had bonded and began working together but a third was beyond rare. The more experienced hunters knew it was a problem, but Newby smiled cockily as he stepped towards them. The vampires snarled. As Giant stepped forward a creak came from the top of the stairs. As No-One and Words turned and looked up the stairs, two more vampires began to descend. They too were older vamps. None of the hunters had ever seen this before and there was nowhere for any of them to retreat to.

Newby began firing as the three that had come through the roof sprung forward. Giant tried to swing his axe but one of the vampires tore it free from his grasp and threw it into the corner of the room. The older vampires moved with a greater speed. Newby wasn't used to it, so his shots went wild. Normally the hunters would team up on an older vamp and surround them or in perfect circumstances, they would attack stealthily and kill them before they were found out for being in the nest.

Words and No-One got ready as the other two vampires descended the stairs. Drool dripped from their fangs and their fingers and nails had grown into claws. Words grip tightened against his now drawn hunting daggers and No-one held his sword with both hands. Neither man dared look over their shoulder to see how their comrades faired. They each knew that a glance away from the vampires could be their end.

The tallest of the three vampires in the basement dove at Newby and grabbed him by his left wrist. It snapped his wrist with a flick of its fingers, picked him up and tossed him across the room. Newby smashed into the stone wall and fell to the floor where he didn't move. Giant who now face the three vampires alone began swinging his axe back and forth, more to keep the distance than anything else.

As Giant was swinging, the two vampires at the top of the stairs sprung on No-One and Words. Words drove both of his daggers through the vampire's chest but knew it wouldn't kill it. It was the best he could do with the time he had. He let go of both daggers at once, bringing his hands up to prevent the vamp from getting to his neck. No-One had speared the other vampire through the stomach but also knew this was but an inconvenience for the vampire. Wasting no time whatsoever, he had pulled the knife from the back of his jeans and began repeatedly stabbing it through the vampire's skull, screaming in the vampires face the whole time he was stabbing. One stab through the brain would have sufficed but the rage and adrenaline had taken over.

Giant was having a much tougher time keeping the other three vampires back. He couldn't make a concerted attack on any of them without giving the other two an opportunity to attack and overpower him. His size was helpful against the older vampires but nowhere near enough to defeat three of them single handedly.

***

As Psycho crept through the upper floor, all was quiet. He could hear the commotion in the basement but knew that his team would dispatch anything that was down there. He would continue making sure the other rooms were vampire free then join them. Each room he entered stunk of decaying flesh and there were parts of human bodies scattered everywhere. Vampires weren't the type to clean up after their self's and generally if they were found, they dispatched whoever found them, so they had little fear of being caught.

With each new room he waited for one of the blood suckers to jump out on him, brimming with excitement of the battle ahead. As he approached the last room at the end of the hall, he was guessing that all the vamps had been hiding out in the basement of this nest, which wasn't all that unusual. He slowly pushed the last door open, cringing at the loud noise the hinges created. As he entered slowly, there was a dark shape in the corner of an otherwise bare room.

"I've been waiting for you."

Psycho took a minute to place the voice. It was the same voice of the vampire that killed his wife. For the first time in years, he was rendered immobile. The tall vampire in the corner turned to face him. It stood naked, all but for the cloak wrapped around its neck.

"Nothing to say?" It asked him.

All the pain of a lifetime of hurt came crashing down on Psycho. He had been searching for this vampire for years. With it being an elder, he could have used some help from the others. On the other hand, he did want to kill it on his own. Once again, Psycho drew his crossed swords. This time though, he used them to slice a thin line along the back of each hand. The pain would keep him sharp. One of them wasn't leaving this room. One way or another he would honour his dead wife.

***

In the basement the carnage went on. Giant had brought down one of the older vampires and was fighting with a second. His axe had been torn from his hands and he fought the elder in hand-to-hand combat. He was the only one in the team able to do this down to his sheer strength and size. No-one and Words fought the other older vamp, all the lesser mongrels having been dispatched. Each of them, including the vampires were now covered head to toe in blood. The room was awash with bodies. It made the fight even more difficult as the hunters kept tripping over the downed vamps and nearly going down. The vampire that was fighting the two hunters at once seemed to be tiring but so was Giant.

As the hunters and vampires circled each other, they could hear carnage breaking out above them. It travelled through the hole that had been made in the ceiling. They knew Psycho had found more vampires and knew he would be giving them hell. It brought a smile to No-One's face while he circled. He had always had a soft spot for Psycho and although he wished he had stuck with the team; they were each their own man with their own pain and had to do what they felt was right.

Giant grabbed the vampire in front of him by the head and lifted it off the floor. He began digging his thumbs into its eyes to blind it. He knew it would still be able to smell him, but it would be easier to beat. As he felt the pop of its eyes as his fingers entered the sockets it let out a roar. As it screamed into its face, one of its claws came shooting up and grabbed his throat. Just as he was going to release its head so he could grab its arm, it tore his windpipe from his throat. He stayed standing for a few seconds while the vampire brought it's claws up in front of its ruined eyes, before he fell to his knees, then flat on his face.

No-one had seen the vampire kill his friend at the very last moment and sidestepped in and lopped the vampire with the damaged eyes head off. Words continued to stab at the other elder vamp with his daggers. With No-One stepping out, it gave the last of the elder vamps in the basement a chance to focus on Words. It had sprung through the air and torn a dagger from his hand. It landed on top of him, perched like a gargoyle and started swinging its claws in wide arcs and slashing chunks from him. No-One returned to the fight and stabbed his sword right through the vampire's chest. It let out an almighty scream and turned to fight him. His sword remained pierced through the vampire, so he dove for the dagger that had been pulled from Words' hand. As he landed next to it and grabbed it, he spun round and slammed it through the vampire's face as it dropped down on top of him. The dead weight hit him like a tonne of bricks. There was no further attack, which was lucky as No-One didn't have an ounce of energy left. He rolled over as best he could and slid out from under the vamp, unable to even push it off him. With great effort, he got to his hands and knees and crawled over to Words, but he was already gone.

No-One couldn't believe the damage that had been done to his team. He had no way of knowing that they were entering a den with so many elders or they would have planned differently. They couldn't have known as they had never seen anything like it before. His mind flashed back to Psycho, and he knew he had to get himself up, get a weapon and go and see what was going on upstairs. Just as he began to get to his feet something came bouncing down the stairs and landed right in front of him. He let out a gasp and went for his sword. He picked it up quickly and went for the bottom of the stairs. Just as he got there another vampire was descending the stairs.

"Your friend and I had a long history. I think he was distracted with his feelings. He didn't fight well."

"Yeh, well. Psycho lived in his head. You won't have that problem with me. The rest of you are dead. Now it's your turn."

"I think not. I'm older than the rest, smarter, and..."

In that second, the old vampires head exploded, right in front of No-One. Chunks of bone hit him in the face, causing him to stagger back. His feet hit something on the ground, and he went down. It was Newby. No-One had completely forgotten about him. The kid had dragged himself through the carnage of the basement floor using his one good arm and then took aim at the older vampire. While he was delivering his monologue, Newby pulled the trigger twice in rapid succession but there was no need as the first shot had been a direct hit and blew the vampire's head to pieces.

No-One quickly turned and surveyed the room and stairs. There was nothing left moving. It was just him and the kid left.

"Thank you." Was all No-One could think of to say.

"You're welcome old man."

They both got their bodies sat against a wall to catch their breath.

"They all dead?" the kid asked, having been unconscious for a large part of the fight.

"Yeh, it would seem so. I can't believe they are gone. We've spent years together. We always knew it could come to this but... I just never throught it would be today."

"They went out the way they wanted. Killing these evil fucking things."

Both were quiet for a while and then No-One stood up. He turned and reached his arm out to let Newby grab his hand with his good arm and yanked him up. Saying nothing else, he turned to the stairs and began to ascend them.

"Oh, one more thing," the kid said.

"Yeh?"

"I want a better name than Newby, now!"

"You got it kid! Maybe we work it out another time though."

"Na, I've got it. Call me Billy. Billy the Kid."

"You like westerns?"

"Na, but I like Billy the Kid, and I think after watching you old guys fight, that I'll stick to my guns."

The End

Chasing Moonlight

By

Greg F. Gifune

He swept into the room like a tornado touching down in a library, his sudden presence disrupting what had been an otherwise quiet conversation in the burned out shell of an apartment Bonnie called home these days. All black leather and drama, the heels of his dark boots clacking the floor, white teeth flashing in contrast, the biggest goddamn gun I'd ever seen in one hand and a plastic bag filled with yellow capsules in the other. "Tamer of the beast," he said, waving the gun at me like a bit-player in an old western. "And enough speed to wake the fucking dead."

Bonnie rolled her eyes. With a sigh, she forced herself to her feet and moved quietly across the room to a boom box propped on an old cranberry crate in the corner. With a press of a finger Soundgarden was singing a familiar tune. She fired an unpleasant glance in Priest's direction, then slid her eyes back over to me and smiled, her narrow hips swaying seductively, arms at her sides, fingers snapping, head thrown back, long razor-straight hair dangling to near the middle of her back.

The sunburst tattoo encircling her navel caught my attention like it always did when she wore half-shirts, and I suppressed a light laugh, reminded of a stoned out girl I'd once seen in an old documentary about Woodstock. It was just Bonnie's way, always finding an avenue of escape, if only for a while.

Priest shook his head and placed the pills on what remained of the counter space near the hollowed out kitchen. His black eyes made love to the cold steel in his hand while mine took a break from making love to Bonnie. I watched him now; that swarthy skin and leading man build. That outfit: the long leather coat and matching black pants, a large gold crucifix dangling from his neck like always, brilliant even in dull light against the backdrop of an opaque silk shirt. The Priest was fucking deranged, and he dressed the part, like some Apocalyptic Cowboy conjured in the mind of a comic book artist high on crack.

I stayed where I was, on the floor with my back against the doorframe, a cigarette waiting to be lighted between my fingers, a hunting knife strapped to my ankle and concealed beneath the lip of my boot, visible only from my vantage point. I played a quick game of visual tennis, bouncing my eyes back and forth between my partners, and caught myself wondering how the hell I'd ended up in this place, at this time.

Confronted with sudden images of my grandmother—her sad gray eyes and gentle, bird-like fingers—I remembered how her soft voice could soothe me and her love had cradled me through the early years after my mother died. Those afternoons wandering the

59

fields and dunes surrounding her little cottage near the ocean had deceived me into believing my future was bright and limitless. My mother was a drug addict, pregnant with me at the age of sixteen, back on the streets turning tricks even before I'd learned how to walk and dead in an alley only weeks before her twentieth birthday. My father was some bleary-eyed asshole slinking through the streets picking up teenage girls for pocket change. I guess.

It all seemed so distant now, like a dream fading to black with each passing hour of consciousness, the details swallowed and transformed into the twisted wreckage of harsh reality. The rest—the here and now and all the bullshit—was little more than fate, the luck of the draw...or the lack thereof.

"Sometimes life is long," Priest said, as if reading my mind. He swept back one side of the coat and stuffed the gun in his belt, then came back with a match in the other, struck it against the wall and leaned closer so I could use the flame. "The key is to not believe in time."

I pretended to have some idea what the hell he was talking about while I drew a deep drag on my cigarette and exhaled a stream of smoke at him. "Where'd you get the piece?"

"Let me worry about that." He spun around, his coat billowing as he turned his back to me and approached Bonnie. "You focus on pulling your weight when all this goes down, yes?"

"Yes," I said, although I'm not sure he even heard me.

Priest looked back over his shoulder, and I knew from the look in his eyes he'd seen the spike and tin foil near Bonnie's dancing feet. "How much this time?"

I shrugged. "Enough to keep her happy, the hell difference does it make?"

"And you?"

"What about me?"

"Are you clean?"

"I'm never clean."

Priest didn't say anything, but he knew what I meant and replied with a knowing nod as he strode right past Bonnie and stood at the only window in the place. Hands on hips, he gazed out at the neon lights illuminating the city streets below. Dusk had become night and I hadn't even noticed.

There were days I'd have just as soon killed him as died for him, but we'd developed our love-hate relationship beyond the simple confines of most friendships. He was in charge, like a father to Bonnie and me, a teacher shackled to a single lesson.

Do as I say, do as I do…

We were either too weak or too stupid to do anything else, but the end result was always the same. Priest had the ideas and Bonnie and I executed them. While sitting on the floor watching him study the streets I wondered if I'd live my life like this forever.

Bonnie just kept dancing, eyes closed, body moving like only hers could. It struck me that once, just like the rest of us, she'd been an infant, a baby swaddled in blankets, innocent and wide-eyed. Goddamn, I thought, Priest's right again. Sometimes life *is* long. Too fucking long...

"It'll just be you and me tonight." Priest turned from the window, his previous smile and relaxed demeanor a vague memory. "We'll be back before Bonnie even knows or gives a shit. Get your coat."

I gave my cigarette a pull, held the smoke deep and pretended I wasn't afraid.

It was a chilly night, and the crisp air snapped me into focus the moment we hit the street. I turned up the collar of my jacket and shuffled along behind Priest, who was strutting across concrete with his typical long, arrogant strides. The neighborhood, at least in theory, was residential, but most people wouldn't have been caught dead there once night had fallen. Too many dangerous types milling about. But we *were* the dangerous types, so we moved through the darkness with a comfort and familiarity most people can never know. Besides, The Priest had a heavy rep. Every bit of bad company roaming the city knew who he was, knew what he was into, and knew he was the last guy on Earth they should be fucking with. I was just a scrawny heroin addicted sidekick, a loyal and obliging altar boy to his blasphemous ministry, no longer certain what the hell I believed, or even why. Right and wrong, good and evil, darkness and light—it all blended together when I was with him, and that's the only reason I could block out what we were all about and separate myself from the hideous things we did.

We crossed Lantern Street and trudged up the slope that was Polk Avenue. Most of the streetlights were out—nothing new—and traffic was at a bare minimum. Unlike the rest of the city it was relatively quiet here, the constant buzzing din of city life scarcely audible. As we found ourselves wandering into a better neighborhood, I knew where Priest was leading me, and the knot in my gut tightened. He knew it would be a big job tonight. That's why he'd scored the speed. We had a lot of work ahead of us, which meant we'd be up most of the night, and he didn't want either of us running out of gas before the deal was done. If I was right I had less than two blocks to talk him out of it.

"We going where I think we're going?" I asked, jogging up alongside him.

"Tonight's the night, Mick."

I hacked up some phlegm and shot it at the curb, ignoring the burning in my chest and the sick feeling tearing through my abdomen. "You sure this is a good idea, Priest? I mean, we've been hitting a lot of yards lately, the cops are gonna—"

"Don't worry about it." He quickened his pace. "We've been working the other end of town. Besides, there aren't enough cops to cover every bone dump in the city."

63

"Yeah, but—"

He stopped and spun around in one crazy but fluid motion and grabbed the front of my jacket. With a quick yank I was so close to him my feet were just barely touching the ground and I could feel his hot breath against the side of my face. Those dark eyes screaming evil, or maybe just indifferent, who-gives-a-shit-about-anything anger, he spoke softly, through gritted teeth. "We've been planning this for weeks and you're going to pull out *now*? This is the big one, Mick. No more nickel and dime bullshit, this one's the fucking motherlode. You want to stick that shit in your arm for the rest of your life? You want that for Bonnie, or do we make enough cash in one night to get both of you into rehab and a fresh start someplace nice?"

I wasn't surprised he'd left himself out of the equation. If the job worked and he moved the goods we thought we'd find he'd get the bigger cut and be in leather coats, gold crucifixes and high-price whores for years. "Let me down, man," I gasped. "I can't breathe."

"In or out, Mick? I ain't got time for games."

"In," I managed.

He loosened his grip before carefully lowering me back to my feet, then he glanced around like a street corner drug pusher to make sure we were still alone before smoothing his hair with gloved hands.

"Did you scope it out this afternoon?"

"Yeah." He sighed, his expression hinting he felt bad about getting physical with me. Like all the times before. "I already hid the tools down by the tree line."

We covered the next block and a half without exchanging words or glances. All I could hear was the thudding of my own heart, the shifting of Priest's coat and the sound of his boots clacking pavement.

The gates were large and ornate, the heavy chain and padlock dangling from them ruining an otherwise Gothic, ancient look. Beyond, darkness blanketed sprawling grounds; rows of headstones and the ghosts I was certain always watched us with helpless, disapproving eyes. The thick curtains of night masking the details of what lay ahead reminded me of my own apprehension, and how it always managed to filter out the voices whispering in my ear, distracting me, at least for a time, from what should have been relentless guilt and shame.

Priest drew a deep breath and scaled the fence with the grace, skill and strength of a commando on a night raid. I fought off a shiver and checked the street again, but we were still alone. He dropped down on the other side and stared at me with those moist black eyes, and I felt the cold steel in my hands, my own weight shifting as I struggled to climb the gate.

Teetering at the top, one leg within the cemetery grounds and the other still dangling in the sane world, I turned and looked out over the enormous spread. Near the back of the yard was a small hill, atop which sat an ornate tomb cradled in a half circle of small trees. This grave was different than the others that had come before it. Priest had done the research; he'd studied the records. Beneath the fancy window dressing were more than dirt and bones and a few filthy trinkets. This time we already knew that what was waiting beyond the boundaries separating this world from the next would yield more profit than all the others combined. I looked down at Priest—so eager and edgy like he always was when we did this—and remembered how he'd promised this job would be our last. Sitting in the cool dark night, perched aloft the gates like some gaunt and sickly bird of prey, I watched the tomb through sufficient moonlight, convinced I would never again go to such lengths to survive. As I swung my leg around and dropped down into the night I couldn't help but wonder why the fuck I even wanted to survive in the first place.

By the time my feet touched the ground Priest was already off, jogging up the hill through a maze of stones. The bend in my arm ached and I felt sick in the pit of my stomach. Wiping sweat and hair from my eyes, I followed him, already picturing myself back with Bonnie, finding the warmth only her body and my weakness could provide.

I stood a few feet from where lawn became concrete as the Priest slipped behind the trees. The tomb was at least six feet high, book-ended by two small guardian angels sculpted from granite, and on the ground before me a crucifix chiseled into a slab of white rock offered a path to the sealed door. The omens and sentinels created to ward off those like us seemed such a grand and elaborate waste. Just like me, they were powerless against the Priest.

We'd first seen the tomb on one of what Priest called our *scouting missions*. While the other stones were packed into neat rows—assembly line death markers—this one stood alone at the summit of the small hill in the oldest and one of the wealthier cemeteries in the city. The flamboyance of the grave itself signaled whoever had been buried there had obviously been well off, and that gave Priest the motivation to investigate its history.

Records revealed the person buried there in 1922 was Malcolm Jersavitch, a long-time resident of the city who had first emigrated from Europe in the late 1800s. For the first time in years Priest went to a library and found Jersavitch had been an aristocrat of powerful standing in both business and the upper echelon of city social circles. The newspapers reported his servants had found Jersavitch dead in his mansion on the north side of the city but had offered no further detail. Some of the considerable funds from his estate had been used to construct a costly and elaborate tomb, where Jersavitch was laid to rest.

Until tonight.

"Come on," Priest said, stepping from the shadowy trees, his arms cradling various tools. "We're fighting daylight here."

I nodded and took a pick and shovel from him. The tools were new—always stolen for each job and then destroyed afterwards—and heavier than they appeared. Priest walked across the granite crucifix slab to the tomb door, dropped the rest of the tools to the ground and removed his coat. He was blinking rapidly and twitching now and then, so I knew he'd already popped a few pills, and I watched as he removed a small vile of acid from his pocket and carefully poured it along the sealed door. A hissing sound and a bit of smoke wafted from the stone, loosening it for our coming efforts.

Somewhere far away a siren blared and faded, swallowed by the distant sounds of the city after nightfall. My knees felt weak and I wanted a fix bad, but I did my best to ignore it, focusing instead on one of the angels on either side of the crypt. It looked so serious, this angel, not at all like the serene and joyful images I'd grown up seeing in books and etched in stained glass. This angel was frowning, as if aware even all those years before upon its creation, it might be staring down someone like me.

The sharp crack of a pick slamming into stone broke my concentration and turned my attention back to the task at hand. I leaned the shovel against one of the angels, gripped my pick as hard as I could, and took up position on the other side of the sealed door. We

68

worked together for what seemed like hours, smashing away bit by bit at the aged stone, stopping only when the intrusive headlight specters of cars passing along the street nearly a hundred yards away broke the delicate balance between moonlight and the dense surrounding darkness.

With bandanas cinched tightly around our noses and mouths, we jammed shovels as deep into the broken seal and behind the door as we could, and then, leaning our weight against the handles, tried to wrest it free from the crypt. When the enormous block of stone finally gave way and fell, actually snapping in the middle before crashing to the ground, it landed with such force the entire area shook.

Even with my nose covered I could smell the sudden gust of stale death billowing from the opening. I turned away, eyes tearing.

Priest tossed his pick aside and leaned forward, hands on knees as he tried to catch his breath. His hair was mussed, his face and neck bathed in sweat. He looked over at me, a smile creasing the bandana and a glint in those opaque eyes.

I glanced at the chunks of fallen stone at our feet, certain I'd keel over and pass out any second, then peered through the still swirling dust and stone particles seeping from the darkness beyond the opening.

Priest grabbed his coat and slipped it on, straightening himself up as if preparing for a fucking date. "Let's go see what we got," he said, tossing me a flashlight.

He stepped over the quarter door still intact, and into the tomb. For some reason I followed him, even then feeling something more than the usual guilt and morbidity our actions always generated.

"Jesus!" Priest snapped, jerking to the side and waving his flashlight up above his head. His outburst scared me worse than it had him, and I backed up a bit, training my light on the same area. A single silver crucifix dangling from a thick chain attached to the ceiling of the tomb hung only inches from the entrance, and apparently Priest had walked right into it. Enough of the beam cut a path through the darkness to illuminate his eyes, and for the first time since I'd met him I saw fear. "Didn't see it hanging there," he mumbled. "Fucking thing startled me."

I nodded, moved by him and swung the light around toward the back of the crypt. A lone casket of wood sat in the center of the hollow tomb, a brown leather Bible placed atop it. I looked back at the Priest, noticed he didn't have his pick, and knew I'd be the one opening the fucker. "You okay?"

He swept the Bible away instead of answering me and examined the coffin more closely. "All that fancy shit outside and they put him in a fucking pine box?"

I could've sworn I actually heard him chuckle, and maybe it was just nerves, fear, repulsion, or my own

70

addictive demons whispering in my ear, but at that exact moment in time I felt like killing the bastard.

"They nailed it shut at least," he said. Stepping back a bit, he motioned to the casket. "Crack the sonofabitch."

The smell grew worse as I raised the pick over my head and crashed it into the wood. It splintered and gave way easily, and by my third swing Priest had already begun tearing away the newly formed planks and tossing them aside, slowly revealing what resided inside.

It was claustrophobic, dark, and musty here, the arched stone walls surrounding us only making it worse. I dropped the pick, yanked my flashlight from my back pocket and swung it around. "Christ all mighty," I said, or only thought, I couldn't be sure which.

What had once been Malcolm Jersavitch was lying in the bare coffin, his mostly skeletal remains gawking at us, arms outstretched and hands with overgrown fingernails that more closely resembled talons frozen forever in a clawing motion. Most of his hair remained, attached to the skull in long stringy tendrils—as if pasted there after his death—and one sunken and what appeared to be mummified eyeball still sat within a socket, the other filled with dirt and dust. His jaw was set open and revealed rows of large grit-covered teeth, as if he'd been screaming at the time of death. He was dressed in a formal black suit and overcoat, a large medallion around his neck.

71

I'd seen my share of corpses long dead, but I'd never seen anything like this.

"Priest—"

"Go outside if you have to hurl."

"—the man was still alive when they put him in here."

He stared at the remains for several seconds before offering a response. "Yeah," he finally said through a sighed, his voice muffled by the bandana. "That kind of thing happened a lot back then. They must've thought the fucker was dead. That's why they used to bleed people, just to make sure they were really gone. Didn't nobody wanna wake up buried."

"Well, this guy did. Look at him, man, he was fucking screaming and clawing at the lid." I moved the light away and ran a shaking hand through my hair. "There's something fucked up about this, Priest, there's something—"

"Bring the light closer." He crouched down and leaned over the body. I did what he said and immediately saw what he'd noticed. A ring with an enormous red stone was displayed on one bony finger. "Holy shit, that's a ruby, Mick. Look at the size of the motherfucker!"

I watched as Priest reached a gloved hand inside and wrenched the ring free. He wiped it clean as best he could and I trained the light on it. He looked up at me and grinned. "What did I tell you, man? What the *fuck* did I tell you? Look at this, it's—Jesus, between this and

72

the—" He only then seemed to remember the medallion. Lunging for it like a cat pouncing on a field mouse, he yanked it free with such force the gold rope chain snapped. "It's solid gold, Mick. Fucking jackpot!"

"All right, cool, but let's just get the fuck out of here, okay?"

Priest struggled to his feet, leering at the items in his hand, his chest heaving with each excited breath. "Even moving this on the black market, you got any idea how much we can get for these?" He laughed, his bandana ballooning out from his mouth and stirring the dust that had all but settled. "We're talking fifty grand at least. That's thirty my way and twenty for you and Bonnie."

I nodded and glanced out the opening behind us. "Yeah, great, let's go, man."

"Hold on." I felt him press the jewelry into my palm before he turned back to the coffin. "Let's see what else old Malcolm took with him."

I jammed the items into my pocket while trying my best to keep the light steady. I needed to get the fuck out of there. I needed to get away from this death and back into the fresh air. I needed to get high.

I don't know why this one was so different from all the others, but for some reason I started thinking about my grandmother. Somewhere far from here she was buried, and I caught myself wondering how I'd feel if a couple of pieces of shit like me and the Priest desecrated her resting place the way we were disturbing this one.

Fighting off images of my grandmother's sweet face and loving eyes, I focused on Priest, who was tearing open the corpse's shirt at the collar. "He might have something else around his neck," he mumbled.

It was then that I noticed something odd about the shirt. Priest had pulled open the topcoat and suit jacket and the collar as well, and the portion near his chest was a different shade than the rest. I stepped closer, tightening the beam. "Look at that."

"What?" Priest said, eyes darting across the body in the hopes I had located another bauble. "Whatcha got?"

I forced a swallow and nearly gagged, battling a plethora of thoughts and solutions suddenly flooding my mind. The light quivered in my trembling hand, my palm so slick with sweat I thought I might drop it. "Look at his shirt!"

Priest turned and gazed at it, and then it hit him too. "What the fuck?"

"That's *blood*," I said.

"What did they...cut his throat?"

I swept the light from one end of the tomb to the next, my panic slowly forming a logical conclusion. "Priest, what if all this stuff—the big tomb all off by itself, the guardian angels and the big crucifix outside, the one hanging in here, the Bible on top of the casket—what if all this shit ain't here to keep people like us out?"

Priest stood up slowly, his eyes never leaving me. "Hell you talking about?"

His face blurred through the tears welling in my eyes. "What if all this was put here to keep him *in*?"

"You're out of your mind," he said, but his voice held none of the arrogance it had earlier.

"They cut his fucking throat, Priest," I heard myself say. "Then they stuck him in here, sealed it off and laid out enough stuff to keep him from getting out. Look at him! He was still *alive*, man! Still alive after they cut his fucking throat!"

Priest seemed to think about what I'd said for a few seconds then waved an angry hand at me, as if swatting the words from the stale air between us. "That ain't possible."

"I'm out of here."

"Hold up," Priest snapped, strutting closer and suddenly remembering his image. "Okay, maybe they *did* murder this guy. They cut his throat and he froze like that, so what? Who gives a shit? This is the way to go from here on out, Mick. It's these kinds of rich fucks we have to raid, and we'll be set in no time, but you can't go getting all spooky on me."

I'd heard what he said but didn't want to believe it. No matter how much we pulled down, no matter how depraved and twisted and evil our game got, the Priest was never going to let me go. "You said this was the last one."

75

"Nah, a couple more like this and we'll be set for the rest of our lives."

There was more than death and fear wafting all around us in that freshly opened tomb. An evil had joined us. An evil so hideous—so tangible and real—you could feel it, taste it, smell it with each invading breath. It pulsed through my veins with a ferocity I had never known previously. More than the beckoning voice it had once been, intent on luring me to heroin and crime and away from every goddamned thing I'd ever truly believed in, this demon wanted more, needed more, demanded more.

Much more...

"Okay, Priest." I offered a subtle nod, held the light still, and reached behind me for the pick, feeling as if I were being pulled down beneath the granite tomb floor into the moist and suffocating earth, entangled with worms and maggots and all else that resided there. Slimy entities swarming over me, filling my mouth, scurrying across my eyes, slithering in my ears and laying eggs across what remained of a brain riddled with disease. "Okay."

***

In the dream it's snowing. Not a heavy snow, but a slow, fluffy and drifting snow, a peaceful kind of snow. In the open field it seems odd, these fat tender flakes sprinkling across such bright and diverse flowers. The dream is bright and vivid and alive, almost like right after you mainline and a stoned mind calls the shots. Bonnie is there with me, lying in the field and cradled in my arms, but they're strong now, like before they'd become bruised and black and little more than a network of track marks. We aren't cold at all, and the flakes tickle our eyes and noses, and Bonnie keeps giggling and catching them with her tongue. But just the way a shark seems to smile right before its eyes go black and it tears you apart, nirvana becomes agony in the beat of a heart.

I'm watching the Priest hunched over the coffin. I'm swinging the pick and the snow turns crimson. He is turning in time to see it coming; swearing and staring at me in disbelief, staggering back and going for the gun in his coat as the pick connects with his throat, bursting it in a tearing, crunching spray of blood and spittle. And then he's falling, collapsing forward onto the casket, gurgling and gasping but still breathing, the blood from the wound gushing, pouring into the coffin and across the corpse over which he is now draped. While he dies, I pull free the knife from my boot, plunge it into the center of his back again and again—twenty, thirty times—however many it takes for the wheezing and groaning to stop. And then the Priest is gone, carried away on snowflakes swirling all around me in a whirlwind, stealing life and giving life, birth and death exploding as one in a dust devil of blood and tears.

***

I stood in the doorway to the bathroom, watching Bonnie lean against the sink with her back to me. I'd gotten home just before dawn but it was already dark again, and I realized I must've slept the entire day. Her eyes, encircled with dark rings, shifted and met mine in the dingy mirror. "Where's the Priest?"

When I offered no answer she returned her attention to the syringe in one hand and the small length of rubber tubing in the other. On the lip of the sink was a used book of matches and a soiled spoon. She fastened the tube with one hand and pulled it tight with her teeth, watching the vein fill and strain. "Is he dead?" Her eyes found me again. "Did you kill him?"

I watched her without response.

Bonnie stabbed the vein, pushed the hammer then pulled it back, the syringe releasing the heroin before backing up with blood. She hunched into a slumped shouldered posture, her eyes struggling to remain open as it hit her system. Pulling free the tube, she let it fall into the sink before turning and facing me, a dreamy smile creeping slowly across her face.

"We're leaving," I said. "Tonight."

"Yeah? Where we going?"

"We're leaving the city. For good this time." I let the doorframe support me. "You won't need that shit ever again."

"You gonna make me all better, Mickey?" Her lips curled away from her teeth and she laughed lightly before flopping down onto the toilet. She was already gone, only she didn't know it yet. "You gonna make me all better?"

I left her there and moved back into the living room. A small duffel bag was resting against the counter in the kitchen holding every fucking thing we owned, but that didn't even matter anymore. Standing by the window in his long leather coat, staring out at the neon sky, he didn't say a word or acknowledge my presence at all. It was like I wasn't even there—never had been, never would be—and I wondered if this was the way it would play out from here.

Moving hesitantly, I slid up beside him and looked out at the night. In a flash of fear and panic the Priest's life had been forfeited, but his blood had also given it. As he died another who had been entombed to save the world had been reborn, and now the fruit of this harvest, cloaked in the same garb, almost looked like the sonofabitch in sparse light.

He reached out to me, the ruby ring returned to its rightful owner brushing my cheek as his talon-like fingers delicately stroked the fresh wounds in my neck. He smiled at me the way one might consider the unaffected simplicity of a child, his brilliant yellow eyes cutting clear through to whatever was left of my rotting soul.

79

I looked up at my new charge—Malcolm Jersavitch reborn—and realized things wouldn't be any different than when we'd been with the Priest.

I'd be chasing moonlight the rest of my life.

The End

A Cold Morning on Lake Dark

By

Michael Bray

The Man dropped the heavy chain into the boat, the old wood creaking in protest. He paused for breath, realising he wasn't as young and healthy as he once was. Time, it seemed, had started to eat away at him. His tired exhalations fogged in the icy air, making tiny plumes before evaporating into the dark. It was one of those bitterly cold nights, and especially here at the lake, the wind bit hard. The water was black and sinister as it lapped around the ankles of his waders, the shoreline, a rough crescent of pebbles scattered with wispy weeds was silent and deserted.

The Man looked into the boat to the boy cowering at the bow. Mouth taped, hair and face streaked with drying blood, eyes wide as he stared at his captor. He was no older than eight years old, possibly younger. His hands were shackled and attached to a second pair which bound his feet. The Man squinted at the sky. There was still work to be done. The Boy, wearing dirty jeans and a thin red t-shirt, shivered as he watched his captor work.

The Man returned to shore, following the length of chain he had not yet put into the boat to a concrete breezeblock. The chain was wrapped around it dozens of times, the two becoming one single entity. He picked up the breeze block, grunting as his joints protested at such heavy work, boots sliding across the pebbles underfoot as he returned to the boat and dropped the breezeblock into it.

He glanced to The Boy, who stared at the breezeblock and chain, which in turn were attached to his shackles. Even so young, realisation appeared in his eyes. The Man ignored it.

'Now you stay there. No sense trying to run. Those shackles and that block mean you won't get far. I won't be responsible for what happens to you if you try it, understand?'

The Boy nodded and lowered his eyes. The Man stared at him for a few lingering seconds, then returned to his truck, which was parked close to the entrance to the lake. It was November, and there would be no tourists to interrupt his work. It was too cold to swim, and there were no locals who lived anywhere close to the lake. It was almost perfect. The Man opened the door to the truck, grabbing a pack of cigarettes and a lighter from the dashboard. He lit up, the orange ember incredibly vibrant in the darkness. On the passenger seat, a folder sat open, inside, a collection of aged newspaper clippings with various sensational headlines.

COLD LAKE KILLER STRIKES AGAIN!

BODY FOUND. COLD LAKE KILLER SUSPECTED.

COLD LAKE KILLER: 26th BODY FOUND.

WHO IS THE COLD LAKE KILLER?

The Man grunted and closed the folder. None of them understood, and he was in no position to explain. He closed the door to the truck and walked back towards his prisoner. Taking a long drag from his cigarette, he tossed it in the water, then pushed the small rowboat free of the bottom into the lake, climbing in far less gracefully than his younger self would have. The Man took his seat at the stern, picking up the oars and guiding the boat deeper into the opaque night. Behind them, the shoreline had already been swallowed by the dark. He rowed towards the middle of the lake, eyes never leaving the boy who shivered and stared back at him.

'Ya know, this is the deepest lake in the country. Coldest too. That's where it gets its name, Lake Dark. Even in the Summer, it's not advised to swim too far out. Undercurrents will take ya, even if you're a strong swimmer. Yeah, dangerous place this, despite how peaceful it looks.' The Man said. The boy stared at him, shivering where he was curled up at the bow.

'There's an old story that somewhere in here is a bomber from World War Two. Shot over France and came down when it was trying to limp back to base. Still, nobody knows for sure. Probably just a story someone made up one time. People make up all kinds of stories about this place.'

The Boy squirmed, still shivering. Subconsciously, the man pulled his yellow raincoat closer to his body. 'I feel that, kid. Cold tonight. Do you smell the rain in the air?

It might be flat calm now but once that wind starts blowin' between those hills....'

He shrugged without finishing the thought. The Man's shoulders ached as he rowed, but the exertion was making the cold easier to bear. He could feel The Boy's eyes on him, hopeful. Pleading. The Man stared beyond him, keeping focused on the task.

'I can feel you glarin' at me, and I suppose that's your right. Fuck, you probably think I'm some kind of monster, don't ya? A cruel and heartless old bastard. Well, truth is, maybe I am. Suppose the older I get, the more I do this, it gets easier. Fact is, I'll sleep just fine tonight after all this is over and done.'

The Boy stared, defiance mixed with anger. The Man laughed. 'Well, if looks could kill I'd be a goner right now. Still, I suppose If we were in opposite positions right now, I reckon I'd be glarin' at you much the same way, so fair's fair.'

The Boy moved position. The Man stopped rowing and reached under his seat and pulled out a short knife, the edge of the blade sharp and streaked with dry blood. He pointed it towards the boy.

'What did I tell you about sudden movements? Am I gonna have to cut you again or are you gonna sit still?'

The Boy settled down, bringing his knees up to his chest. The Man watched, then, satisfied, put the knife back under the seat and started to row again.

'Don't make this any harder than it has to be for you. You gotta know, there ain't no stopping this. It's gonna happen, one way or another. You can either go bleeding and hurt or be comfortable and quiet. It's up to you.'

The Boy couldn't speak, but his eyes said enough. The man grinned.

'Shit, you look like you want to tear my goddamn head off. Don't blame you, I suppose. I'm not even mad. Sometimes, they act the same as you when it gets to this point. Angry. Defiant, right to the end. Others break sooner, crying and wide-eyed so bad you can almost taste the fear. Gotta say, I respect the defiance.'

The Boy stared at him, eyes pleading. The Man looked away into the darkness.

'Always ends the same way, though. Ain't nothing to change that. I don't see that fear in you, not yet, anyway, but I expect I will soon enough. When we get to where we're going at least. Ain't as young as I once was. These trips are taking longer and longer.'

They went on in silence towards the middle of the lake. It started to rain. The Man pulled up the hood of his raincoat. In the front, The Boy continued to shiver, his T-Shift already soaked through and sticking to his skin.

'Just about there,' The Man said. He looked at The Boy, studying his features. 'Weird, I thought you'd be scared by now. You're either tougher than I thought or just plain stupid. Dunno which. Suppose it doesn't matter.'

The Man stopped rowing, pulling the oars into the boat and setting them on either side of him. 'Well, here we are. End of the road.'

The Boy looked at him, eyes wide and afraid. 'You know they've given me a name? consider me a criminal. They class me as a serial killer, which I suppose is fair enough. You're not the first and won't be the last. They call me the Cold Lake Killer. Have you heard of me?'

The Boy stared at The Man, not reacting.

'Can't say I was ever really sold on the name, but it's not like I can just go to the press and ask them to change it, can I? Not after all these years. Eh, well, I don't suppose it matters. Not now. Not for you. Are you scared yet?'

The Boy stared at him, expression impossible to read. For the first time, The Man felt a little discomfort. He wanted the prisoner to feel something, or at least understand the enormity of what was about to happen before the end, otherwise, what was the point in any of it? He took a deep breath, reminding himself that he shouldn't get too caught up in that stuff. Be professional. That was the key. He never used to take such pleasure in his work, but the years surrounded by death and living in the shadows had made him cruel. Society would never understand, nor would it ever have a place for someone like him. As the years went by, the man often wondered if he was still a good person. He was sure he was once, many years ago, but now, he mused, his heart had become as black and cold as the waters underneath them. He had seen too much, *done* too much to ever be redeemed. Either way, that was his cross to bear. His problem to handle in the best way he could.

The Man noticed The Boy looking at him and was angry at letting his thoughts drift. Another sign that age was dulling his senses, and there likely weren't too many more years he could actively do this. He stared at the child, eyes devoid of humanity, words cruel and without pity.

'Cold will take you first. Once you hit that water, it will shock you. Natural instinct is to take a breath. Before you realise what you've done, you're taking in water. No way to push it out, no way to stop it, especially with that block pulling you to the bottom. I've done this a few times now, and I always wonder which one is worse. The cold, or the not being able to breathe.'

He hoped this would scare The Boy, but still, he sat, shackled and defiant. For some reason, it made him angry. 'You understand what's about to happen, don't you? You're going to die here today. Just like all the others.'

He waited, sure that this would get a reaction, but The Boy just lowered his head, staring at his shackled feet. 'Well, time's up. Let's get this over with.' He moved towards The Boy, who flinched away, pushing himself against the frame of the boat. *This* was the reaction The Man wanted. He grabbed The Boy by the arm, dragging him to his feet, the boat rocking as the child kicked and squirmed.

Without warning, the night was gone, the small boat illuminated by spotlights from all around. The Man let go of the child, who retreated to where he had been, cowering against the frame of the bow. An amplified voice broke the silence from behind the spotlights.

'Armed Police. Stay where you are.'

The Man squinted, lifting his hand to cup his eyes to see beyond the blinding light. He could just about see them. Police boats, had surrounded him in the darkness and were now springing their trap.

Rage swelled inside The Man. 'Leave me alone, you don't understand.' he screamed at the faceless enemy.

'Hands up, don't move.'

The Man did as he was told, his stomach tightening, blood hot with anger. This wasn't the way it was supposed to be.

'Stay where you are, we're coming to you.'

Engines from the unseen darkness of the lake fired into life as a larger police rescue vessel was suddenly visible, searchlights illuminating the water. It angled towards the small fishing boat.

The Man knew it was over, and if he was going to go out, then he would make sure he did this last one. He lurched for The Boy and dragged him to his feet, forcing him towards the edge of the boat and the black waters beyond. The Boy squirmed and kicked, muffled screams coming from beneath his duct-taped mouth.

'Stop, let him go.' The voice from behind the lights said, but to The Man, they were inconsequential. They meant nothing. This was what was important. Finishing what he started. It was all that mattered.

The Boy knew what was about to happen, and increased his thrashing. The police boat was closer now, its engines roaring in the silence of the night as it pulled up beside the rowboat.

'Let the child go, this is your last warning.'

The Man did as he was told, instead turning his attention to the breezeblock. He tried to lift it, the sudden movement almost caused the small vessel to overturn, and he lost his grip on the block. He knew that once the child was overboard, there would be no saving it. He tried again, managing to lift the cumbersome brick to stomach height. It would only take a few steps to have it overboard, and no matter what the police did, it would take The Boy with it.

There was an explosion of sound, a singular gunshot piercing the night.

The Man fell back, stumbling over and landing hard his head connecting with the seat at the bow, fire in his shoulder, breezeblock landing back on the deck of the boat, breath expelled from his body in an instant. He could see the blood welling up through the hole in his raincoat. He tried to get up, ignoring the pain, ignoring the sounds of them coming. They were climbing onto the boat now, two of them, but still, he had to try. He got to his knees, but it was too late. They were already onboard. One pointing a gun at him, the other going to check on The Boy. The Man screamed. 'You don't understand, I have to finish – '

It was no good. They were already on him, pushing him back, placing cuffs on his wrists. The Man started to cry. Great sobs of anguish. The officer patted The Man down, checking for weapons. He found only his keychain. He turned to the other officer in the boat who was with the child and handed the keys to him. 'See if any of these open those chains.'

'Don't do it,' The Man said, as the Officer dragged him to a sitting position.

'Got it, this one fits.' The officer at the bow said as he released the shackles from the child. 'Hey, it's okay, kid. We're going to get you to safety.' The officer pulled off the tape covering the boy's mouth. Free at last, the boy smiled.

The officer stared, eyes wide unable to comprehend what he was looking at. The old man lay on the deck of the boat, hands cuffed, unable to do anything but observe, knowing that for all of them, it was already too late. The second officer managed to fire off two shots towards the child before he was taken. The Man lay there, listening to the sounds of flesh being ripped from bone, blood spilling against wood. Screams and chaos, gunshots and then, silence. It took only moments. Seconds, possibly. The Man no longer had any concept of time. All he had left was fear, a thick bitter thing he could taste in the back of his throat. Footsteps approached the man from the police patrol boat, and he knew well enough what it was. The Boy hopped into the rowboat. He was covered in blood, eyes defiant. He grinned, his mouth impossibly wide, row upon row of needle-like teeth, still covered with blood and chunks of flesh revealed behind his lips.

The Boy spoke, his voice far beyond his childhood years. 'I lied to you earlier,' The Boy said, his voice a wet growl. He stood over the man. 'When you asked me if I'd heard of you.'

The Man, remembering the defiance The Boy had shown earlier, now tried to do the same and glare without fear, but without success. He was terrified and it was clear to see. He wanted to scream, but somehow swallowed it down.

The Boy opened his mouth, the width impossible, jaw splitting at the bottom like that of a snake, showing even more teeth lining the throat. This time, The Man did scream. There was no way to stop it. He was still screaming as The Boy approached, maw oozing with blood and saliva.

Morning.

Officer Dale was just about to clock off the night shift when he was asked to swing by Lake Dark. A sting operation had stopped responding, and he was the only available unit that could go take a look. He drove down the curved lane towards the lake entrance, skeletons of leafless trees overhead exposing the overcast early morning sky. Beside him in the passenger seat, the new kid, Jenkins, stared out of the window. It was a right of passage for the newbies. Work the night shift for a while, get used to the procedures, and then get out into rotation. There were still nights to work of course, but it went from every week to one in five or one in six if they were fully staffed.

'Holy shit,' Jenkins muttered as they turned left and the lake opened up in front of them. In that instant, Officer Dale went from half dreaming about ending his shift and getting some sleep to being fully awake and alert. He stopped the patrol car, scanning the scene in front of him.

'What do we do,' Jenkins said. The kid was scared, and Dale didn't blame him. He was scared too.

'What do you think? we need to check it out.'

'We're going in there?' Jenkins said, adams apple bobbing in his throat.

'It's our job. We need to secure the scene. Come on.'

'Are you sure about this?'

Dale *wasn't* sure, but he couldn't let the kid see it. 'Course I'm sure. Come on. We need to secure this before anyone sees it.'

Dale got out of the patrol car, wishing he had a gun, and hoping the pepper spray and Taser would suffice if there was trouble. He walked onto the pebble shoreline of the beach and let his eyes drift across the scene. There was a small rowboat pulled up the beach, blood covering the chipped white wood. Out on the lake, a police patrol boat bobbed on the water. Even from the beach, Dale could see at least two bodies slumped over the side, one hand in the water rocking with the motion of the boat.

'Fuck me,' Dale whispered.

His eyes were drawn to the truck parked a little further up the shoreline. The Man was on the hood, head lolling against the windshield, mouth open in a never-ending scream. His beard, which was once grey, was stained crimson. Both his eyes had been plucked out, and his arms spread to the sides as in mock crucifixion. His entire stomach cavity was empty, his intestines wrapped around each wrist and tied to the wing mirrors of the truck. In the gravel where the man's feet hung in front of the number plate, the rest of his innards, still slick and glistening, were gathered.

Dale had never seen anything like this in his eight years on the force. He turned to Jenkins, who stared open-mouthed, skin taking on the colour of the leaden sky.

'Go back to the car, call it in. Get crime scene down here. Hell, get all available units on scene now. Hurry.'

Jenkins nodded, almost stumbling over his own feet as he ran back to the patrol car. Dale moved around the horrific scene in front of him, angling around so he could see inside the open driver's door. On the seat, he could see a folder filled with news clippings. Dale approached so he could see. His eyes skimmed over the articles within.

'Holy shit, no fucking way,' he muttered to himself as he moved closer. Beside the folder, an old leather wallet sat on the seat. Dale put on his gloves and took it out, opening it as Jenkins returned. He was still pale.

'They're on their way,' Jenkins said, unable to take his eyes from the gruesome display on the front of the truck. 'What do we do now?'

'First thing is, keep your distance. We can't risk contaminating the scene. Go back to the car, run a name for me, see if you get any hits. I think it's our guy on the front here.'

'Okay, what's the name?'

Dale referred back to the driving licence inside. 'Last name, Van Helsing, first name Abraham.' Definitely looks like our guy. Come on, let's get out of here. We don't get paid enough for this bullshit.'

Dale put the wallet back on the seat, then he and Jenkins retreated back towards the patrol car. Already, in the distance, the sirens were growing closer.

The End

The Proposal

By

Lee Mountford

Shaun felt numb. The news he'd received had not yet fully registered, but never the less its magnitude still weighed heavily within. He had been given months. Not years, not even a full year, but a few months. Hardly enough time to scratch your arse in today's world yet that's all he was left with.

He swung his car into the nearest available space, switched off the engine and sat in silence for a moment. He tried contemplating what he could do, what he *should* do, where he should go and whom he should talk to, but his mind was in no mood to be thinking logically. All he could think of was to go home, go to bed and see if things look differently in the morning. He looked out from his car, into the night, to the run down high-rise building across the street. His place was on the top floor; the penthouse suite of shitsville. Not much but it was his, for a few more months anyway. Shaun gave his head a quick shake, hoping but failing to clear his mind. The news was slowly working its way into his reality; his world had been turned upside down. Again.

Shaun lethargically heaved himself to the top of the stairs and ambled to his door, digging around in his pockets, to retrieve his keys. The lock clicked and the door glided open. There she stood; wearing a smile so confident and seductive it caused Shaun's stomach to knot instantly. He hadn't seen Amber in over a year, not since that night, the night she told him what she had become. Of course he didn't believe a word of it at the time, but the physical demonstration that followed was a little hard to ignore. Her dress sense had changed dramatically from the woman he once knew. The new Amber was certainly not afraid to flaunt her features. She ran a glistening tongue over her blood red lips and her smirk intensified. She looked better than ever.

'Well hello Shaunie, surprised to see me?' She asked. Realizing the look of surprise was plastered across his pale face, Shaun tried to gain some form of composure. The last thing he wanted was to seem weak to her. To give the impression he wasn't in control. He did the best he could to shrug nonchalantly.

'Not surprised, just disappointed.' Shaun spat and, after he did, he noticed her air of confidence wane ever so slightly. He'd hit a nerve and he was glad of it. 'Why are you here?'

'I think you know why.' She retaliated immediately, quickly regaining her state of confidence. It was true, Shaun knew exactly why she was here, but how did she find out so quickly?

'I guess news travels fast with your kind?' He hissed and strode fully into his apartment, slamming the door behind him. Shaun was careful to keep his distance, not wanting to get to close to her.

'I've been keeping an eye on you Shaunie.' There was a predatory look in Amber's eyes, the same look that Shaun had noticed the last time they met, a look that was never there when they were married.

'Have you now?'

"And I know about you're condition.'

'Good for you.' Shaun was struggling to fight back his bubbling anger. The news he'd received was bad enough, but coupled with her presence here - it was becoming too much. 'And how do you know about that? I've just found out myself.' The remark caused Amber to chuckle condescendingly.

'Oh Shaunie, a girl like me has contacts you know. You have no idea how many people want to become what I am. And it's so very easy to keep those puppets dancing on a string for me. Teachers, lawyers…even doctors.' She laughed again and Shaun felt himself go red with rage. 'Silly little thing, I knew about your condition before you did.'

'And you came here to rub it in?' He growled through gritted teeth. Amber's expression grew serious, and there was a hint of something in her eyes. Something Shaun had not seen in a long time.

'Thirteen months ago I came to you with an offer Shaun. Do you remember?' It was a stupid question, what happened that day was impossible for him to forget. The day Amber, his wife, revealed to him what she had willingly become. The day he found out she had turned her back on humanity, the day he found out everything he believed in was false, the day he found out his one true love had become a fucking vampire. No, this was not the sort of thing that would slip ones memory.

'I remember everything I need to about that day, you traitorous bitch.' There was venom and pain in his voice.

'You're still angry I see. That's fine. But would you care to explain who it was that I betrayed?'

'Me!' Shaun yelled, his fists now clenched.

'I offered to turn you, but you were too small-minded to see what was being given to you. It was you who turned your back on me! I wanted you with me Shaun, to be like me.'

'To be like you?' Shaun's eyes were tearing up, all of his erratic emotions were slowly becoming too much to handle.

'We're not monsters Shaun. We do what we need to so we can survive, just like you do, just like any form of life does. And you have no idea how free we are.' Her face broke into a smile and her eyes slowly closed in a dreamy state as she carried on her explanation. 'How free and how powerful. We live how we want, for as long as we want and no one can stop us.' Amber's eyes then opened and locked onto Shaun.

'Tell me that doesn't entice you. Surely now, considering your impending death, you can see just how weak, breakable and pathetic you are. I can change that.'

Shaun turned his head and averted his eyes, not wanting to look at this thing before him. The person he once loved now made him sick to his stomach. What was worse was the fact that her offer was so very tempting. His own weakness only served to intensify his anger. He had rejected her offer before, but things were different now. The God he had loved and believed in had decided to remove him from the earth – while creatures like this, who were a stain on his very name were allowed to live on and on.

'One more chance Shaun.' She whispered. 'You can take it or you can stay here and rot.'

Shaun erupted and charged the hateful vixen. It was as if his body was acting on instinct, every molecule of his being wanted to hurt this woman, this monster, hurt her like she'd hurt him. He didn't get the chance. In an instant Amber changed, revealing the true from of what she had become. Her eyes flashed yellow like a golden flame and animal-like fangs bore from her snarling mouth. She grabbed the charging Shaun by the throat and with inhuman strength threw him powerfully to the floor. With blinding speed she was atop him, straddling him and pinning him to the ground. One hand still clenched his throat as he thrashed wildly. Amber increased her iron grip, cutting off his airflow, and clamped her thighs tightly, trapping his arms by his side and rendering him totally at her mercy. Tears began to roll from Shaun's eyes.

'Do you see what I mean now?' She snarled, her grip tightening even more. 'Do you see how weak you are?' Shaun's crying continued as he broke down completely.

'I'm scared!' He wailed and Amber's hold eased. 'I don't want to die.' He continued in a tear-filled plea. The animalistic glare in Amber's eyes began to fade, revealing remnants of the compassionate person she once was. 'I just don't.' Shaun repeated.

'You don't have to Shaun.' She soothed, almost kindly, and caressed his face. 'Just let me help you.' He held his breath, cautious and afraid of what he was submitting to.

'Okay.' He said, 'help me.'

Amber smiled upon hearing this, a genuine and relieved smile. 'Thank you.' She whispered and leaned in. Shaun felt her fangs penetrate the skin on his neck, and then a numb euphoria took hold as she began to drink in his life essence.

Amber; The woman he once loved. The same woman who had scorned, hurt and broke him, and shown him just how weak and vulnerable he really was. And the same woman who was now giving him the power to inflict the same hurt and pain on her that she had inflicted on him. The power to destroy her. The power to get revenge.

Shaun smiled as he slipped from consciousness for the last time as a human being.

The End

Heroes

By

Richard Chizmar

<u>1</u>

I've always watched him. Secretly. From the time I was a child. Watched the way his eyebrows danced when he laughed. The way he lit his pipe or handled a tool, like a magician wielding a magic wand. The way he walked the family dog; bending to talk with it or ruffle its fur, but only when he was sure no one was watching. The way he read the newspaper or one of his tattered old paperbacks, peering over the worn pages every few minutes to keep me in check. The way his eyes twinkled when he called me "son."

I've   always   watched   him.

<u>2</u>

The detective's name was Crawford and when he disappeared into the crowd, I wondered for what had to be the tenth time tonight if I was truly insane for trusting   him.

It was Thursday, December 21, and Baltimore-Washington International Airport was suffering under the strain of thousands of holiday travelers. A river of lonely businessmen and women, sweatshirt-clad college students, and entire families flowed by North Gate 23, blocking my view of the exit tunnel. I remained sitting on one of the orange-padded seats in the waiting area while Crawford tried to get close enough to look out the airport windows. Our man was due on an 8:30 p.m. flight from Paris--a private charter--so the computer screens all around me offered no news of its arrival.

I stared at the clock on the far wall. It was almost time. Months of research and planning were about to come to an end. My stomach felt like it was bubbling over and I was tempted to duck into the bathroom. Instead, afraid to leave my seat, I popped another Tums and waited for it to dissolve under my tongue.

Crawford reappeared, trailing behind an overweight couple who were moving with the grace and speed of a pair of hermit crabs. I could see by the expression on his face that the news was not good. I'd hired Ben Crawford, a Philadelphia-based private detective, two months earlier. He'd been the only one of the half-dozen detectives who'd been recommended to me who was willing to take my case. A fifty-thousand-dollar certified check--half payment in advance--had   sealed   the   deal.

We made an odd pair. I stood over six feet tall but tipped the scales at only one-sixty. Crawford, on the other hand, could best be described as a human stump; only five-four, he weighed in with one hundred and seventy pounds of compressed muscle. His arms and legs strained against his clothing, and like many other muscular men of his size, he more waddled than walked. Despite my edginess, I smiled and almost laughed aloud at the sight before me: the waddling detective   and   Mr.   and   Mrs.   Hermit   Crab.

"What's so damn funny?" he asked, moving his coat from the chair next to me and sitting down.

"What . . . oh, nothing. Nervous tension, I guess."

He checked his watch. "The plane just landed. It'll   be   another   ten   minutes   or   so."

I nodded, my throat suddenly dry, my stomach tightening   another   notch.

Now it was Crawford's turn to smirk. "Hey, take it easy, you're white as a sheet. Don't worry, he'll be on that plane." He glanced at his watch again. "Another couple of hours and it'll all be over. Trust me."

I nodded again. I trusted him all right. I had no other   choice.

3

104

Twenty years ago, when I was seventeen and still in high school, each student in our senior English class was assigned to write a paper about the person he or she most admired. The class was a large one and the list of heroes was long and impressive: Martin Luther King, Abraham Lincoln, John F. Kennedy, Joe Namath, Willie Mays, John Glenn, and dozens of other famous figures. I was the only student who chose to write about his father. A nine-page tribute. My father cried at the kitchen table when he read it. Stood up and hugged me real close. I'll never forget that day. Never.

4

Even in the dim light, I could see that he was a striking man. Tall. Elegant. Draped in a fine black overcoat, dark slacks, and shiny, zippered boots. His face contrasted sharply with his slicked black hair and dark apparel. Deathly pale flesh appeared almost luminous in the airport lights, and sharp, high cheekbones seemed to hide his eyes under his forehead. Eyes as dark as midnight.

"Jesus," I whispered.

"Yeah, I know," Crawford said, leaning close enough that I could feel his breath. "He's something, ain't he?"

Before I could answer, the detective stepped past me and met our visitor at the side of the walkway, away from the swelling crowd. I stumbled blindly after him, not wanting to be separated.

"It's a pleasure to see you again, sir," Crawford said.

Neither man offered forth a hand, and I noticed that our visitor's hands were covered by black leather gloves. He nodded and smiled. A quick flash of teeth. Like a shark. A chill swept across my spine.

"As promised, I am here." His voice was mesmerizing; his words soft and melodic like music. I wanted to hear more.

"Yes, you certainly are," Crawford said, sounding infinitely more civilized than I had ever heard him. "I trust your trip was satisfactory."

"Indeed, it was quite comfortable. But, my friend, I long for the journey home, so may we continue on quickly?"

"Yes, yes, of course." Crawford eased me forward, his fingers digging into my arm. "This is--"

"Mr. Francis Wallace," he interrupted, smiling again. I felt a wave of nausea rush forward and began to sway. The detective's fingers tightened on my arm again. "I have crossed an ocean to make your acquaintance."

"I . . . I really must thank you for coming here," I said. I looked helplessly at Crawford. "I'm not sure I believed him until I saw you walking up the tunnel. I was so terribly afraid that I had been wrong all this time."

"It is not necessary to thank me, Mr. Wallace. I have thought about this moment many times since your friend's visit to my home. I admit, initially, I was wary, hesitant to come. But yours is such a strange story, such a strange reason for my journey. My decision to come here was much easier than your decision to seek me, I trust."

A pack of giggling children skittered past us, brushing the man's coat. He cringed and turned to Crawford. "I am ready to proceed now."

The detective led us through the busy airport, outside into the bitter December air, to his rental car in the upper-level parking lot. The traffic on the interstate was moderate. We drove north in silence.

5

It was my father who stood at my side on my wedding day, and I by his, eight months later, when Mother passed away. Barely a year later, and it was my father again, his arms around me, who broke the news to me that my precious Jennifer had been killed in an accident. It was the worst of times, but still we had each other.

6

melting. I played with the zipper on my coat for a long time before I looked up.

He was staring at me.

"You okay?" he asked, his breath visible in the chill air.

"I don't know." I took a deep breath and looked over my shoulder at the front door, which our visitor had disappeared into just minutes earlier. "I planned this for so long . . . thought about it for so long, but I don't know. I'm still not sure it's right."

He shook his head. "Listen to me, I gotta admit that I thought you were a genuine nutcase when you hired me. Offered me a hundred thousand to go find this guy and convince him of your little plan. Hell, I only signed on because I was short on cash and long on bills."

He stood up and inhaled on his cigarette. Began pacing the walkway. "I mean, I thought he was a fantasy, something made up for the movies and books. But the more you showed me about this guy--the papers, the files, the photos; all dated over hundreds of years--and the more time I spent around this house, getting to know you and your old man . . . the more I understood. You've gone to an awful lot of trouble, Wallace, an awful lot. Now, you don't know me very well; not well at all, in fact. But if you're asking for my opinion of all this, I think you did good. I think you did damn good."

A soft thud sounded from inside the house, and I jerked around.

Crawford kneeled at my side, pointed a finger at

me. "You did good, Wallace. Trust me."

"Oh, God, I hope so."

7

I don't watch my father anymore. It hurts too much.

Ten months ago, on a Friday night, he forgot my name. I had just returned from the grocery store with the week's supplies--he was no longer able to drive himself--when he called me into the den. The television was on the wrong channel and he couldn't figure out how to work the remote control. He looked me straight in the eyes and said, "Charlie, could you please turn on HBO?" I laughed, thinking he was acting the smart-ass, one of his favorite pastimes.

But later at dinner, he asked, "Charlie, pass me the salt and pepper."

I looked at him; there was no humor in his voice, no mischief in his eyes. "Dad," I said, scared, "who is Charlie?"

A confused expression creased his face. "What the hell kind of question is that?"

"Just tell me who Charlie is, Dad."

He laughed. "Hell, buddy. Don't you even remember your own name? We served in the war together, Charlie. You were my wing man, for Christsakes."

It came to me then. Charlie Banks--my father's

best friend, dead over fifteen years now.

It was a long night, but the next morning, everything was back to normal. I was his son again, Charlie Banks completely forgotten.

But I could see the signs then. No longer able to drive, arthritis, failing eyesight and hearing, advancing stages of senility . . . the list continued to grow as each month passed.

As did my own depression and anxiety. I remember someone once said that there is nothing sadder, nothing more heartbreaking, than watching your hero die.

They were right.

It was during that time I decided I couldn't let that happen.

The snow was falling harder now. The narrow streets were covered, neighborhood yards of dead grass just beginning to glisten a beautiful white.

I was standing by the rental car, nervously running my bare hand over the cold metal. The two of them stood huddled together on the porch, Crawford's cigarette aglow. The man had emerged from the house several minutes ago, but the detective had insisted on talking to him first. Alone. I'd trusted him this far, so I'd agreed.

Five minutes later, twenty minutes before midnight, they finished talking and walked to the driveway.

Crawford pulled me aside and said, "Your dad was sleeping like a baby. Just as we planned. There was no pain, no surprise."

I closed my eyes, nodded my head. "Thank you," I whispered. "Thank you so much."

"It's been my pleasure," the detective said, reaching for my hand. "And I mean that. Now, don't worry about anything. I'm going to get our friend back to the airport and back on that plane. You get inside." He waved at me from the car. "I'll be in touch."

Before he joined Crawford, the man laid a hand on each of my shoulders, touched a single gloved finger to my face. "Immortality is a rare and wonderful thing, Mr. Wallace. But it is not without its failings. It will not always be easy. Cherish this gift, protect it, as I know you will, and you and your father will be truly rewarded."

Tears streamed down my cheeks. I opened my mouth to thank him, but the words did not come.

He held a finger to my lips. "Say nothing. I must go."

I watched the car back out of the driveway, pull away into the night, its brake lights fading to tiny red sparks in the falling snow. I looked at the second-floor window--my father's bedroom--then at the front door. A snowflake drifted to my lips, and I opened my mouth, tasted it like I had done so many times before as a child. I looked skyward and caught another on my tongue. Then, I started across the lawn, his words still echoing in my head.

Immortality is a rare and wonderful thing. God, I hoped so.

The End

Devil in the Snow

By

Nick Roberts

The airplane came to a crisp stop on the defrosted runway. Caleb stepped onto the icy ramp as the Alaskan cold chewed through his North Face jacket. He zipped it up to his nose, but the exposed areas of his face stung within seconds. The forty-yard walk from the runway to the tarmac felt like a trudge through a pissed off walk-in freezer.

The distant sun hovered over the mountain range beyond Ted Stevens Anchorage International Airport. He learned that the sun rose here at 10 AM and set around 4 PM this time of year, and it looked like it was on its way down. He walked faster as the breeze began to push him sideways.

The glass doors slid open. Caleb entered and breathed a sigh of warm relief. He unzipped his jacket and removed his hood, searching for the baggage claim area. The clock above Starbucks read, "3:02 PM." That meant it was 7:02 PM back home. He rubbed his eyes and yawned. Jetlag fogged his brain. It had been a long trip from Appalachia to Alaska, and he lost four hours during the flight.

Caleb's mom had dropped him off at Yeager Airport in Charleston, West Virginia at 4:45 AM to make his 6:00 AM flight. On the twenty-minute drive to the airport, she had gone over the same spiel he'd heard ten times already. She kept saying things like, "A month away from all this is just what you need," and "You're twenty years old. If you don't clean your act up now, it's only going to get worse," "Staying on an Air Force base with your brother will do you good. Look at how much it helped him," and most pointedly, "I'm done, Caleb."

She could frame it anyway she wanted, but the end result was the same; she was tired of his drinking and drug use and wanted him out of her hair for thirty days. She had pointed out that he started and stopped college twice already, which, if that wasn't for him, meant that he needed to get a job.

He worked at Pizza Delight, starting out as a pizza topper before moving up to assistant manager. But after the cash register count came up short on more than one occasion when he ran shifts, the store manager finally shitcanned him. He was out of his apartment within the next month and back in his old room at his mom's house.

When she posed the question (that was really an ultimatum) about going to spend December with his older brother by two years, Rich, in Anchorage, Caleb flipped. He had immediately called his dad to see if he could move in with him across the state just until he "got back on his feet." His father, who had even less tolerance for his son's dilemma, told him, "Screw staying a month. Why don't you just enlist yourself and do something with your life? It worked for your brother." Sure, Rich had been just as bad—if not worse—than Caleb before he enlisted, but there was no way Caleb would thrive in that environment.

Suddenly, the month mandate from Mom didn't sound so bad compared to signing his life away to the military. When they had pulled up to the curb of the airport, Caleb just opened his door, grabbed his suitcase out of the trunk and didn't look back. It was only when his mom had stopped him and given him a hug and reassured him that this was for his own good that he felt anything less than angry. She had said she loved him, and he had muttered it back as he left his hometown behind.

This was only the second time Caleb had been on an airplane, but he had never ridden by himself. The flight itinerary began with departing Charleston at 6:00 AM for Chicago, Chicago to Denver, and then Denver to Anchorage. All in all, it was over thirteen hours of waiting, flying, eating airplane snacks, getting pissed because he couldn't order in-flight booze, and failed naps.

Now, staring at the clock atop the closed Starbucks sign, the gravity of his situation finally set in.

"Fuck," he muttered to himself and slunk toward one of the airport maps.

He made his way toward baggage, passing a massive stuffed moose wearing snow goggles and a toboggan. There weren't nearly as many travelers here

115

as there were in Denver and Chicago, but he avoided eye contact with all of them just the same. The thought of having to force a smile or, God forbid, participate in small talk repulsed him.

Caleb's stomach rumbled. Burger King, Arby's, and Subway—each fast-food storefront looked tastier than the last, but he'd wait and see what Rich wanted to do for dinner. The one highlight of his trek through the tarmac was the moving walkway. He'd never been on one of those before the Chicago airport and looked forward to each new one he encountered. For one brief reprieve from what he considered an exile, he allowed himself to feel like a world traveler.

When Caleb finally made it to baggage claim, he scrolled through Twitter as he waited on his bag to appear on the conveyor belt. His phone notified him that his battery was less than ten percent. He put it in his pocket right as his maroon suitcase wobbled out through the square in the wall and made its way to him.

"Excuse me," he said to an elderly woman standing in the spot where he wanted to intercept his bag.

She smiled and stepped to the side as he snatched the heavy suitcase with one arm, nearly tipping over.

"You got it, son?" a tall man with a cowboy hat and a flannel shirt asked.

"Yeah, yeah," Caleb said as he jerked the suitcase to the floor, extended the handle, and rolled it to wherever his brother would be waiting for him.

The last time he'd seen Rich was at their dad's house eight months ago. They were all standing on the porch. Caleb and his dad were smoking cigarettes, but Rich had recently quit and even began jogging to get in some kind of shape before being sent to basic training. Rich reached out and hugged his younger brother. Caleb hugged him back, never once considering that Rich would ever be in any real danger.

He remembered thinking that that stuff just happened to other people. Rich would serve his time honorably, and safely return home. They broke from their hug, and Rich and their dad got in the Jeep Wrangler and headed toward Beckley, West Virginia for processing before being shipped to bootcamp. At the time, Rich was a little under six feet tall, lanky with shaggy hair, and had a bad habit of slouching.

An upgraded version of Rich now stood near the airport exit. He was wearing a tight thermal shirt and a toboggan with his coat draped over his arm. Caleb couldn't believe how much muscle he'd put on. His shoulders looked like softballs, and he had pecs for the first time in his life. But even with Rich's new build, it was the way he carried himself that impressed Caleb the most. His older brother stood upright, firm, and proud.

Rich smiled as soon as he saw Caleb walking toward him wheeling the suitcase. He marched over to him and squeezed him against his chest. For the first time in months, Caleb felt happy.

"I missed you, man," Rich said.

"I missed you too. You look like a soldier."

They broke their embrace.

"That's what drills will do for you, I guess."

Rich smiled again.

"I'm so glad you're here."

Caleb half grinned and nodded his head. Rich put his hand on his brother's shoulder.

"Look, Mom didn't ship you up here as a punishment. You know that right?"

"Yeah, I know."

"Do you?"

They made eye contact, and Rich had that no nonsense look in his eyes.

"You gotta get your shit together. Hangin' out with me up here won't be so bad. I promise. Hopefully, you'll be a in a better space a month from now."

"I hope so."

Rich patted him on the back and then put on his jacket.

"Alright, let's get out of here. You hungry? Wanna grab a bite before we head to the base?"

"Sure."

"Cool. Let's go. There's a McDonalds right down the road."

"Sounds great."

***

As they drove down the expertly plowed roads of downtown Anchorage in Rich's new Ford F-150, Caleb couldn't believe how different the city looked compared to what he had been expecting. He thought the plane would land on a bobsled track that fed into a town of a few frozen buildings and houses, covered in snow and surrounded by mountains. He was only partially correct.

The city—the size and quantity of the buildings—impressed him. It wasn't some tucked away village in the frozen tundra; in fact, it resembled Charleston, the capital city of West Virginia. But instead of the forested Appalachian Mountains surrounding the city, it was the snowy white and purple peaks of the Chugach Mountains.

"Do you want to go through the drive-through or eat inside?" Rich asked.

"Inside is fine with me if you don't care."

"Sounds good."

Caleb noticed the golden arches a few blocks ahead. He looked out his window at the street vendors who had shops set up at almost every intersection. Many of them had fur coats and hats and stood under tents pedaling their wares.

"Are those Eskimos?" he asked.

"Yep. But they prefer to be called Inuits or just natives. They sell all kinds of cool shit here."

"They must freeze their asses off standing out here all day."

Rich laughed.

"Dude, these people know how to live up here. December's not even the coldest month. January is where it really drops, but you'll still see them standing out here, snow or shine."

"Even after it gets dark?"

"Oh yeah. They build fires and grill fish and stuff. People don't stop living just because it gets dark earlier."

Caleb tried to see into each vendor's tent as they passed. One with sculptures and little figurines caught his eye.

"Do you care if we check out a few of them after we eat?" he asked.

"I don't care. It's Friday. I'm off tomorrow. We can do whatever you want. I do want to show you around the base tomorrow though. I think you'll dig it."

"That'd be cool."

The brothers ate their Big Mac combos and reminisced about the dumb stuff they did as teens. Caleb did his best to update him on all the best new movies and TV shows that had come out recently. They discussed their favorite new songs, dissecting certain lyrics by Eminem or Kendrick Lamar. Rich told him all about boot camp and how it was not like *Full Metal Jacket* (Caleb's only frame of reference). He also described how life was different on the base, how you had to salute certain people depending on what uniforms each other wore, but what impressed Caleb the most, was how cheap everything was at the BX—the on-base shopping center where everything was tax free.

"Have you thought about what you're gonna do when I go to work Monday?" Rich asked.

"Not really. What time do you get off?"

"I'll be home around 5:30."

"I'll probably sleep in and binge some shows I've been meaning to watch until you get home."

"I have weights and a treadmill in the basement if you want to incorporate that into your routine."

Caleb took a sip of his Coke through the striped McDonalds straw and thought about it.

"Yeah. I think I will."

"Really?"

"Yeah. I want to look like you."

Rich smiled.

"We can pick up some pre-workout and supplements at the BX on the way home."

"Mom didn't send me with very much money."

"Don't worry about it. I've got you covered on whatever you want, booze excluded."

"Really? You don't party anymore?"

"I didn't say that. Drinking is sort of a job requirement up here, even more so overseas."

"So, what's the problem?"

"For this month, I'm not gonna drink and neither are you. What kind of big brother would I be if I didn't lead by example?"

Caleb couldn't believe this was the same guy who talked him into smoking his first joint when he was thirteen and Rich was fifteen.

"You're gonna relax, regroup, exercise, get your head on straight, and hopefully figure out what your next step in life will be."

Caleb saw the seriousness in his brother's eyes, but the look wasn't scornful or stern; he sounded more like a coach or a motivational speaker. He actually believed his brother, and a euphoric wave of hope washed over him. Maybe he could do it. Maybe he didn't have to be a twenty-something slowly progressing ino the downward spiral of addiction and alcoholism.

Rich scarfed down the last bite of his burger as Caleb chewed his fries. Apparently, the military had sped up his brother's chowtime.

"Eat up if you want to hit the street vendors," Rich said. "The base is twenty-six miles away, and the BX doesn't stay open all night."

Caleb chewed as fast as he could and listened as Rich described all the different types of "badass" aircrafts he'd seen so far.

***

It was almost dark as the two of them walked the salted sidewalks, scoping out the street vendors. Some sold fur coats and hats, others only one of the two. One vendor was speaking broken English to a potential customer, going over the benefits of the boots he was trying to sell. Caleb looked in another and saw anything one could make with leather hanging from twine ropes.

The two brothers stepped onto the next block and passed a robust woman polishing one of the signs in her tent that was filled with home décor carved from wood, polished rocks, and even alabaster, but Caleb had yet to spot the one that had initially piqued his curiosity.

And then he stopped.

"This is it."

"Oh yeah," Rich said as the two of them entered the large tent. "This does look cool."

Shelves filled with figurines of all shapes and sizes lined both walls of the tent which led to an old man in a rocking chair behind a small wooden desk. A metal box sat on top of the desk beside a calculator. He puffed a cigar and smiled as the two men entered.

"Hello there," he said without getting up.

"Good evening, sir," Rich said.

Caleb just smiled and nodded as he looked at the single shelf of figurines behind the man. Several expertly crafted sculptures displaying varying degrees of grotesqueness were lined up from one side of the tent to the other.

123

"Air Force, you are," the old man said to Rich and then turned his attention to Caleb. "But you're not. You two look alike. Let me guess...you're up here visiting your big brother."

Caleb nodded.

"You hit the nail on the head," Rich said.

"What brings you two by my shop?"

"My brother..." Rich began, but Caleb cut him off.

"Those figurines," he said, eyeing the ones behind the man.

The old man slightly turned and looked at them as if he'd forgotten they stood there.

"Ah, yes. Do you like those?"

"Yeah," Caleb said, looking from one to the next.

"Which one do you prefer?"

He scanned them twice. There was a serpent-like creature that reminded him of something from an H.P. Lovecraft story. A yeti stood between a grinning forest witch and a cyclops with crab legs. A hairy beast that looked like a hybrid of a wolf and a bear was fixed in a silent howl. They were all great. He was about to settle on the yeti when he noticed something hanging from twine above the shelf. At first, he thought it was a miniature bird house.

"Wait, what's that?" Caleb asked.

"What's what?" the old man said without turning around, his friendly charm waning.

"*That*," Caleb said, pointing to the dangling piece of art.

It was solid white, but not a figurine like the others with its tiny teapot shape. It had a humanoid face with its jaws wide open. Rows of sharpened teeth lined the top and bottom of its mouth. Two monstrous canines extended out as sharpened fangs. Even though it was just a head, two white wings extended out from behind in mid swoop.

The old man slowly turned around as his smiled faded. He looked up at it.

"Oh, that," he began. "That's not for sale."

"Then what's it doing in your tent?" Rich asked with that big brotherly tone in his voice.

"The twine must've come loose. I had it tied up higher. It's not for customers. I keep it here for me. Sentimental value, you could say—aside from being made from whale bone."

"What is it?" Caleb asked.

"A trophy," the old man said as his voice trailed off.

"A trophy for what?" Rich asked.

He turned back to face the brothers.

"You really want to know? It's a bit of a long story, but one I don't mind telling because I don't get the chance to do it much."

"I'd love to hear it," Caleb said.

"OK then," the old man began. "My tribe has seen darkness, way back when I was just a boy of

125

twelve. This was fifty years ago, you see. People were getting dragged away in the middle of the night. Men, women, and children—it did not matter. We'd find their remains the next morning.

"Hunters would go out during the day and return empty handed. Men would stand watch at night, but still the beast would sneak into our village and steal one of us as silently as it arrived. The hunters were useless. I was never a hunter, however. *I* was a trapper, you see?"

"What kind of a beast was it?" Rich asked. "A bear? Wolf?"

The old man hesitated and met Rich's gaze.

"Yes...a wolf," he replied and then continued his story. "My younger brother and I devised a plan. We would sneak out to the edge of the village. My brother would sit at the base of a tree—he was ten at the time—and I would hide in the tree branches above him with my weighted fishing net. When I saw it—the wolf—coming, I was to alert my brother as it approached him. He would move around to the other side of the tree, and I would drop the net on it and trap it. I would then climb down, and we'd grab the fishing spears we'd hidden on the other side of the tree and stab it to death. Not the greatest plan, I know, but we were children."

"So, what happened?" Caleb asked.

The old man smiled solemnly.

"We put our plan into action, and the devil—the wolf—showed up. I saw it prowling across the snow. I was supposed to alert my brother, but I froze the moment I saw it. By the time I got the nerve to warn him, it was too late. It had already spotted him, and I'd never seen anything like it. I fumbled with the net and fell forward on the tree branch. I heard my brother scream just as the branch snapped in half, and I plummeted with it to the earth. The last thing I heard before I passed out was the wail of the, uh, wolf.

"I woke up in my father's arms as he carried me back to the village. I had never seen my father cry until that point. I found out later that when I fell, the branch pierced the beast through the heart, but the devil had already ripped out my brother's throat. The village was safe, and my brother had died protecting it. We were heroes to everyone but our parents. The elders burned the remains of the beast at dawn and put its ashes in that very urn hanging above me. They gave it to me as a trophy. And so, that's how a trapper killed what the hunters could not, even though it wasn't pretty."

"That's quite the story," Rich said with a hint of condescension.

The old man glared at him.

"How much do you want for it?" Rich asked.

"I'm sorry. It's not for sale."

"Really?" Rich began. "You're gonna build us up with that whole story—one I'm sure you've got reserved for all these trinkets—and still play hardball?

Let's skip the song and dance and just give me the price."

The old man crossed his arms and leaned back in his chair.

"Rich, it's OK," Caleb said. "I can get one of the other ones."

"You want that one the most though, right?" Rich asked without taking his eyes off the old man.

The old man matched Rich's gaze and nodded his head.

"You're a good big brother," he started. "I wasn't. I didn't deserve that trophy in the first place. But you, you're a soldier...a *hunter*. My little brother was the brave one. He should've been the one to get it. Not me. I led him down the wrong path, and he died because of it."

The old man stood up and turned around. He pulled a knife from his sheath and slit the twine, removing the dangling string from the urn. He placed it on the table beside the metal money box. Caleb leaned over and examined it from every side.

Eyes like golf balls bulged out of their sockets. It had taut skin stretched across pointy cheekbones. Its gaping mouth looked like it could snap like a bear trap at any moment, draining the blood from its helpless prey.

"It's amazing," Caleb said.

"Like I said, this was meant for my younger brother, not me. You're *his* younger brother. If you want it, it's yours," the old man said.

"No, seriously. How much?" Rich asked.

"The price has already been paid for it. You just do a better job looking after your brother than I did for mine, OK?"

"OK then. That's a promise."

The old man tore off a piece of brown wrapping paper from the industrial sized roll, wrapped the urn, and put it in one of the gift bags. He handed the bag to Caleb.

"Here you go, young man."

"Thank you, sir," Caleb said.

He couldn't remember the last time he'd called anyone sir.

A laughing man and woman stumbled into the tent, each holding a bottle of local Alaskan brew.

"Whoa, check out all this shit!" the guy said, and the girl giggled.

"Let's head home before it gets completely dark," Rich said.

"OK," Caleb said and then looked back at the old man. "Thanks again."

The old man just said, "Keep it, and yourself, safe," and then stood up to help his new customers.

***

The last sliver of sunlight illuminated Elmendorf Air Force Base as the brothers stopped the truck at the front gate. A guard in uniform stepped out of the shelter, which was only slightly bigger than a toll booth, and walked over to Rich's window. Rich rolled it down and showed the guard his ID.

"You get uglier every time, Johnson," the guard said, referring to Rich by his last name, barely checking the ID. "And who do we have here?"

"This is my brother, Caleb. Caleb, this is Airman First Class Garcia."

Caleb leaned forward and held up his hand.

"Pleased to meet you, Caleb. *You* can call me Gabe. Sorry you're related to this one over here."

Caleb forced a chuckle. He watched Garcia hand Rich a clipboard and a pen.

"You know the drill for visitors."

"I know. I know," he said as he filled it out quickly and handed it back. "Hey, we'll be headed back out in probably an hour or so. I want to properly show him the Northern Lights. Will you be here?"

"I'm on a twelve-hour rotation, so fuck yeah I'll be here."

"Try not to fall asleep again," Rich said as he rolled up the window and drove under the opening gate.

They heard him yell, "That was one time!" as they drove toward the housing units.

When they pulled onto Rich's street, Caleb couldn't stop staring at the rows of houses on both sides of the road.

"These are so nice. I don't know what I was expecting, but it wasn't this."

"That's one perk of this base. Each house has four bedrooms, three bathrooms, a two-car garage, and a fenced in yard. This is mine right here."

"This looks like the neighborhood from *The Stepford Wives.*"

They pulled into Rich's driveway. He pressed the garage door opener on his visor, and the door slowly lifted. As they waited, a GMC Arcadia pulled into the driveway next door. A family of four got out of the large SUV.

A guy with short blonde hair stepped out and waved at Rich. He opened one of the back doors and helped one young girl out and then another. They were carbon copies of each other. A short dark-haired woman got out of the front passenger seat, waved at Rich, and then escorted the kids into the house and out of the cold. The man walked across the driveway, his breath visible in the frosty air, and stopped at Caleb's window. Rich rolled it down.

"Hey, buddy," Rich said.

The blonde-haired guy leaned in. He had an easy-going smile and kind eyes.

"What's up Brothers Johnson?"

"Caleb, this is Timmy. Timmy, Caleb," Rich said.

131

"Sup little bro," Timmy said. "Are you freezing your balls off yet?"

"I'm pretty sure I left them in Denver."

Timmy laughed.

"What are you all getting into tonight?" he asked.

"We're gonna unpack and unwind for a minute and then go up to the scenic overlook to check out the light show."

"Oh, cool. Yeah, man. You'll dig the Northern Lights. It's something you'll never forget, yet you'll get tired of it in two days. Odd how that works."

"What are you all getting into?" Rich asked.

Timmy laughed.

"Uh, dinner, bath and bedtime...possibly some sex if we haven't passed out first."

"Good luck with that. Oh hey, did you see the moose again this morning?"

"Fuck yes," Timmy said. "I let Lucky out first thing, and he started barking his ass off. That damn thing was standing on the other side of the fence in the back yard."

"At least he was in your back *yard*. I walked out at 6:30 this morning and it was pitch dark, and he was walkin' across my driveway. He must be doing laps around the complex."

"So, moose just wander around up here?" Caleb asked.

"Yep," Rich replied. "Just like deer back home. You'll see them everywhere. Just leave them alone, and they'll leave you alone. Ain't that right, Timmy?"

Timmy started laughing.

"No, don't pin that on me," he said. "Caleb, me and your dumbass brother killed a bottle of Jager like a month ago. We walk outside to smoke and see the moose. *This* motherfucker dares me to run up to it and smack its ass. I do, of course. Well, I tried. I crept up on it and reared back right when both of my feet slid out from under me. I landed right on my ass, and that moose took off. Damn near trampled me."

All three of them laughed.

The porchlight turned on at Timmy's house. His wife opened the door.

"Are you coming?" she asked.

Timmy tapped the window and stood up.

"That's my cue. I'll see you guys tomorrow. We'll go out to eat, or cook for you or something."

"Sounds good, bro," Rich said and rolled up the window.

"Nice to meet you," Caleb said before the window shut.

He liked Timmy. It was the first time he'd laughed that hard in a while. He carried that smile with him as they drove forward and closed the garage door on the freezing night.

After a quick tour of the house, Rich showed Caleb to his room.

133

"And this is you," he said, gesturing to the spacious room with a queen bed, a dresser, and a nightstand.

Caleb walked in and slung his suitcase on top of the bed.

"I'll let you get unpacked. I gotta take a shit," Rich said.

Caleb smiled.

"OK. Thanks, man."

"Oh, here's this," Rich said as he placed the gift bag with the urn on the dresser and then disappeared into the hallway.

Caleb immediately picked up the bag and pulled the wad of brown paper out of it. He unwrapped it like he was un-swaddling a newborn baby. The white, hissing face stared back at him. He stuffed the paper back in the bag and discarded it, walking over to the bedroom window as he examined the exquisite craftsmanship in his hands.

His finger rubbed across its face, feeling the grooves in the whale bone. The fangs jutting out looked like they'd been sharpened enough to chew through a Coke can. Like a child touching a hot stove for the first time, he pressed the pad of his pointer finger against the tip of the pointed tooth. The fang instantly popped his flesh, and a trickle of blood ran out.

"Ouch!"

He winced and lost his grip on the aged trinket. It fell against the marble window seal with a crack and then toppled to the floor.

"No! Shit."

He bent down to assess the damage, but there appeared to be none. But he had heard something crack.

What made that sound?

And then he felt something on top of the head that hadn't been there before. Some part of the urn had popped loose. It jutted out like a wine cork the size of a pencil eraser. He wondered if this is how they put the wolf's ashes inside it. After debating whether or not to push it back down or pull it out, he chose the latter. With a delicate twist and a pop, he removed a pellet-sized piece of bone and placed it on the windowsill. A tiny swirl of ash bellowed out like dust from the opening of an ancient tomb.

Caleb waved it away, and a black hole stared back at him. His heart started to race, but he didn't know why. It was just the ashes of a long dead wolf inside of carved whale bone. Just as he brought the hole up to his eye to catch a peek at what's inside, he noticed something odd. He stopped and pulled it back.

The blood smear that had disappeared.

"What the hell?"

He looked it over, but it was as white as when he first saw it. His finger was still dribbling blood from the puncture. It didn't make sense. He looked again at the hole in the urn—at the black abyss within—and for reasons he couldn't comprehend, he found himself holding his dripping finger above the hungry hole.

The urn shook with each bloody drop. Caleb raised his head to face the window. He unlatched it at the top and raised it up. A chilling wind took over the room, but he didn't care. He knew what he had to do but didn't know why he was doing it. With the urn in both hands, he held it out the open window, slowly turning it upside down until ashes began to spill from the hole and blow away into the night sky. He shook it empty and then pulled it back in and shut the window.

The plug lay on the sill where he left it. He picked it up and was about to put it back in the urn when he noticed something small written all the way around it. There were three words that he'd never seen before. He said them aloud.

"AUK...TONNGAK...MURUANEQ."

Before the final syllable left his mouth, he took out his phone and did a quick Google translation. Apparently, the words he'd just uttered were Inuktituk, and they translated to: blood, devil, snow. He sat his phone down, pressed the cork back in the urn, and walked it back to its place on the dresser.

"Blood devil in the snow?" he wondered aloud.

His brother's heavy footfalls coming down the hallway broke Caleb from his trance, and suddenly he was staring at the demonic face, baffled at what had just happened.

"Hey, bro. You OK?" Rich asked, walking into the room.

"Yeah. I just got a little dizzy," he said, trying to recall the last few moments, but feeling hazy.

"You've had a long day. Probably just jetlagged and tired. Look, we don't have to go check out the lightshow tonight. We have a month to explore."

"No, no. I'm good. Let me get these clothes put away, and we'll go."

"You sure?"

"Yeah, man," he said, getting irritated.

Caleb unzipped his suitcase and stared at the piles of stuffed clothes, a toiletry bag, another pair of shoes, and some books. He opened the dresser drawer and shoved the stack of pants in it. He grabbed a pile of shirts from the suitcase.

"If you have a Coke or something with caffeine, that'd help."

"Red Bull work?" Rich said with a smile. "It gives you wings."

"Yeah," he chuckled. "Wings would be great."

***

Forty minutes later, and the brothers pulled into a snowy parking lot near one of the many parks in the area.

"There's a lot of cars here," Caleb said.

"Friday night in Anchorage. The tourists flock here to check out the light show, and the Air Force guys do our best to hook up with the tourists. It's the circle of life," Rich said with a smile. "Come on. It's just a quarter of a mile hike up this hill. And grab the chairs out of the back."

After a slippery, zig-zagged hike up the hill, they reached the top. There were clusters of people scattered about, some had fires going. Everyone their warmest hats, coats, and gloves as they bundled together marveling at the sky. Caleb placed both seats in a vacant spot.

"This good?" he asked.

"Works for me."

The brothers sat down and looked up.

"There she is," Rich said.

Caleb had seen pictures of the Northern Lights in school and online, but he saw now that they did them no justice. The night sky was peppered with blazing white stars of an unprecedented clarity, looking almost within arm's reach. Had this pristine view of the universe been the only natural wonder they came to see it would have been enough. But, in front of those brilliant stars were dancing swirls of neon, yellow, and green hues, blending together, in and out in an undulating cosmic painting.

"Wow."

"Wow, indeed. Makes you feel pretty small, doesn't it?"

Caleb only continued to gaze at the greatest light show the world had to offer. A waft of what smelled like high-grade marijuana interrupted him. He looked to his right at a young couple sitting beside a portable firepit, sharing a joint.

Damn, it smelled good.

He looked a little further down the clearing at a group of men, each holding flasks or bottles of liquor. His brain replayed that feeling of that first warm swig of alcohol heating his body from within. But it wasn't booze or weed that he really wanted. What he craved came in a little orange prescription bottle and could be crushed and snorted, obliterating not only the toughest physical pain, but that mental pain as well.

"Caleb," Rich said.

Caleb turned his head to face his brother.

"You OK?"

"I really want to get fucked up."

Rich looked at the surroundings and everyone else who was there with their recreational drugs of choice.

"Shit, I didn't even think about people partying up here. I'm sorry. We can bail if you want to."

"No, it's OK. Really. Just saying that out loud made me feel a little better. I've never done that."

Just as an optimistic grin started to form on Caleb's face, a woman shrieked from further down the clearing. She screamed again, and then a man did as well. The brothers both stood up to get a better view.

"What the fuck is that?" Rich said.

Caleb couldn't believe his eyes. A woman who looked to be in her twenties rose through the air as if being pulled up by a string. He squinted and focused on the shape in the darkness holding the woman. It wasn't a string. It was a winged figure, pale and hairless with what looked like grotesque bat ears.

The creature held the woman around the waste as it sank its teeth into her throat, its wings flapping as it continued its ascent. The man screamed from below as the humanoid creature took one final bite into her throat before ripping her head completely from its bloody stump. Seemingly uninterested in the remains of the corpse, the creature let her head and lifeless body fall back to the earth with a thud.

Chaos ensued on the ground. Dozens of intoxicated strangers ran amuck as the creature floated up there, flapping its wings, staring down at the pandemonium below. Blood that looked purple and pink under the neon lights cascaded down its jaws.

"Run," Rich said, grabbing Caleb by the shoulder.

Caleb watched as the alabaster devil swooped down faster than any eagle and snatched up one of the older men with the flasks. Unless he was mistaken, it was the cowboy guy from the baggage claim area of the airport.

Again, it lifted its prey into the sky, opened its gaping mouth with monstrous fangs and gnawed through the man's throat. With its bite firmly clamped, it gripped the man by the shoulders and spun his body around until his head popped off and the remains rained down.

"I said to fucking move, Caleb!"

Rich jerked his younger brother by the shirt, but Caleb only stumbled and fell on the snow. The creature was the monster on the urn—the monster *in* the urn. That Inuit merchant hadn't trapped and killed a wolf as a child. He'd somehow lucked into slaying a vampire just by crawling too far out on an unstable branch that came crashing down and pierced the creature's heart. It was then that Caleb knew that they didn't burn it. The sun had done that for them. He didn't know how he knew this; all the pieces just came together at once like those brilliant lights twirling in the sky.

The ancient predator radiated menace. This creature was no suave version of Dracula from Bram Stoker's tale, and it was even more beastly than Nosferatu. It dove into the crowd again. This time he arose holding two young women, crying and begging for their lives.

"Get the fuck up, Caleb!" Rich said and grabbed his brother, jerking him to his feet.

They both froze when they saw the pale devil hovering in the air. It was staring at them and smiling. Each one of its clawed hands burrowed into the scalps of the helpless women as it lifted them up until his arms extended out to each side like a crucifix. With a wider, bloodier grin, it smashed its hands together like it was

141

playing cymbals with the women's heads. Their skulls exploded like melons in one forceful blow.

Caleb's get-your-ass-to-safety function finally kicked in, and he sprang to his feet, almost slipping again in the snow.

"Come on," he said when he noticed Rich facing the beast.

"He's coming for us."

Caleb turned back around just in time to watch the devil's wings shoot straight out to the sides, the top of its fifteen-foot wingspan gleamed like a blade in the moonlight. When he looked even closer, he knew that's exactly what it was. The top of each wing was a straight razor going from one side all the way to the other.

In one swift motion, it dove toward the ground and swooped into gliding mode three feet above the ground, slicing through a horde of bodies, torsos sliding off of still standing legs.

"Run!" Rich said, and this time they were both on the same page.

The two brothers bolted to the left toward the trees and down the path, not bothering to zigzag as they had on their way up. Caleb stumbled, but Rich pulled him up, and they kept moving. The horrid screams of the helpless people behind them echoed into the night.

They hit the makeshift parking lot and didn't stop until they were inside Rich's truck. He fired it up and backed out faster than he ever had before. The truck sputtered as he floored the gas and then took off. Caleb struggled to put on his seatbelt as the truck slid when Rich turned onto the main road.

Rich shifted gears and kept checking the rearview mirror.

"What the fuck was that thing?" he said, struggling to catch his breath.

"It's my fault," Caleb muttered.

Rich looked at him.

"What the fuck do you mean?"

His memories had come back to him the moment he saw the vampire. He remembered the vampire urn's fang poking him and drawing blood, the cork that unleashed the ashes, opening the window to free the devil, and then having it all blocked out as if under a spell, which he knew now that he had been.

"The urn from the old man..."

"What about it?" Rich asked, cutting him off.

"It bit me. It made me open it and dump the ashes out the window."

He could feel Rich staring at him.

"Keep your eyes on the road, please."

"The base is just right up here."

Rich guided the truck into the base's entrance and slammed the brakes inches before hitting the front gate. Garcia, still on shift, stood up and flung the booth door open. He started yelling before Rich could lower the window.

"I don't care how drunk you are...don't you ever come speeding up to my gate like that or I'll have your ass!"

"Get back in that booth and call for help right now," Rich said in a tone that made Garcia switch his. "There's something on the hill. It was killin' a bunch of people!"

Garcia cocked his head. His face was a divide of skepticism and concern.

"What the fuck are you talking about, Airman?"

"God damnit, just call for help. People are dead up there."

Caleb leaned across the console.

"It's true. It's a, uh...crazy person."

"A crazy person, huh?" Garcia began. "From what I can see, you all are the only crazy..."

A white blur hit Garcia like a linebacker from Hell. The soldier made a sound like he just got socked in the gut and then disappeared into the night. Caleb peered through the windshield just in time to see the white wings flapping up into the night sky. Garcia's final scream got cut short and then they heard a distant thud as his body fell to the earth somewhere in the darkness.

"Fuck this," Rich said and got out of the car.

Before Caleb could ask what he was doing, Rich had already opened the booth door and pressed the button to open the gate. He got back in the truck and drove onto the base.

"Where do we go?" Caleb asked.

144

"Main building up ahead. We'll get this bastard blown out of the sky."

The creature landed on the hood of the truck with a *THUD*. Rich slammed on the brakes, but it dug its claws into the metal to keep from being thrown off. For the first time, Caleb got a good look at it up close.

It was a hairless ghoul with taut skin that stretched back across its overly skeletal face with its sunken eye sockets, housing two white eyes that glowed in the dark like tiny moons. There were two reptilian slits in the center of its face where a nose should've been. It sneered, exposing its canine fangs that were at least three inches long, and rows of what looked like shark teeth on the top and bottom of its jaws.

Rich couldn't see shit. He swerved to the right and hit the road that led to his house. The creature wobbled a bit and hissed at Rich. Then it locked eyes with Caleb, and at that moment, Caleb knew he was its primary target. It ripped one clawed hand out of the metal like it was going to punch straight through the windshield.

"Hit the brakes!" Caleb said.

Rich did, and the white beast tumbled backward off the front of the truck and rolled onto the road in front of them. Seizing the opportunity, Rich accelerated and drilled the creature just as it got to its feet. Its body rolled up and over the truck, thumping against the metal. It fell on the truck's solid bedcover and fell to the snowy road a second time.

"Woo! Take that, you fucker!" Rich shouted into his rearview mirror.

As they approached Rich's house, he pressed the garage door opener and nearly hit the rising door as he drove under it so fast. He shut it just as quickly behind him.

"What do we do?" Caleb asked.

Rich opened his door and ran to the door to the house. Caleb wasted no time following him.

"We're calling base police," he said as he flicked on the kitchen light.

Caleb immediately ran over and turned the light back off.

"What are you doing? We don't know if that thing is dead or not," Caleb said.

"Good point," Rich said, with a hint of embarrassment that Caleb detected.

Rich felt his pockets for his phone but came up short.

"Oh fuck," he said.

"What?"

"My phone was on the armrest of the chair on the mountain."

"Shit."

"Where's yours?"

"I didn't take it with me. It's on the charger in my room."

Before Rich could make his way to the hallway, he stopped and stared at the pale figure standing on the other side of the living room window. It twisted its head, and its grin slowly widened. Caleb watched with curiosity as it balled up its fist and instead of busting through the glass like he thought it would, the creature used one of its elongated knuckles to tap three times on the window.

Both brothers were statues.

The creature repeated the action but knocked a little harder and then gestured with its head to the front door.

"It wants in," Caleb said. "*No*, it has to be *invited* in, right?"

"How the fuck should I know. You're into that horror shit, not me."

Rich raised his middle finger and said, "Fuccccckkkk offffffff."

Caleb backed him up by saying, "We're gonna leave you out there until dawn and let the sun cook your fucking ass!"

The creature's smile disappeared, its wings expanded, and it took off like a rocket.

"What does it want with us?" Caleb asked. "It killed everyone up there. It easily could've killed us at the booth or in the truck. Why us?"

Rich bit his lip and furrowed his brow and finally said, "Because we have the urn."

"The urn?"

147

"That's the only thing I can think of. What if that urn is like a genie lamp or some shit, and it wants it back."

"Or it just wants to kill me," Caleb said, looking down at his punctured finger, "because I'm marked."

"Well then, I'm not wasting any more time. I'm breaking that shit," Rich said as he began to walk toward the staircase.

A car horn beeped from the driveway next door. Both brothers looked at each other, confused, and then ran to the window. Timmy's SUV door was open, and the interior light was on.

"Oh, shit," Rich said.

They heard Timmy's front door open and then watched him when he came into view walking down his sidewalk to investigate. Rich banged on the window.

"Timmy! Get the fuck out of there!"

Timmy turned to look at the commotion. The creature leaped over the SUV and landed behind him. Before he could turn back around, it picked him up by the throat and dragged him across the snow to the window. It pressed Timmy's terrified face against the window and then motioned again to be let in.

"Timmy?" his wife said from her porch. "Timmy, what's going on?"

Timmy's eyes widened, and the creature smiled. It lunged into the air. The brothers heard it land on the porch next door and then listened to a brief yelp before a full scream could come to fruition. Both brothers jumped back as the creature landed in front of the window again, now holding Timmy in one hand and his wife in the other. Its long, massive hands covered their mouths and muffled their screams.

Again, it motioned toward the front door.

Rich and Caleb looked at each other and back at the creature. The creature grimaced and used its clawed thumb to puncture Timmy's eyeball like a grape, swirling it around inside the socket. Timmy writhed in pain, but the creature kept him quiet.

"Fuck!" Rich said, turning away.

"We have to let him in," Caleb said.

Rich looked at him like he needed clarification.

"It's the only way. If that old trapper man killed it with his brother when they were kids, then we sure as shit have a chance. You give it permission to come in and go grab whatever weapons you have in here, and I'll run upstairs and destroy the urn, assuming that's going to do anything. And then we just tag team it."

"Tag team it?" Rich repeated.

The creature, clearly growing impatient, pulled his thumb out of Timmy's empty eye socket and plunged it into the other one. Timmy spasmed, helpless against the creature.

"OK! Fuck it. We'll tag team it," Rich said, and Caleb nodded. He looked at the creature and said, "You can come in, just let them..."

Before he could say "go," the creature simultaneously dug the claws on both of its hands into

149

the eye sockets of its captives, smiled for a moment, and then ripped off the tops of their skulls. Their half-headless bodies toppled over, and the creature disappeared into the sky.

Rich put both hands on the windows and let out a scream full of primal rage. Something landed on the roof. They both looked up and listened as the creature took heavy steps from one side of the house to the other.

"He's going for the urn," Caleb said.

"Not if I get it first," Rich said and then bounded up the stairs, disappearing into the hallway.

Caleb, completely thrown off by the sudden change in plans, scanned the room for any weapon. He thought back to what the old trapper had said had killed the creature the first time: getting stabbed through the heart. He ran to the fireplace and grabbed the poker.

Rich reappeared in the hallway carrying the urn.

"I got it!"

The ceiling above him exploded as the creature dropped down into the house. Debris of wooden splinters, drywall, and snow rained down on top of it. It stood erect, blocking Rich's path to the staircase. Caleb, standing at the foot of the staircase, felt sick to his stomach knowing that he was about to watch his brother die.

"Rich!" was all that he could say.

"You want it?" Rich asked the hideous devil that looked down at him. "Take it."

He chucked the urn above the creature's head which almost touched the ceiling. It desperately reached for the flying object while Rich lowered his shoulder and speared the creature so hard that he heard something inside it crack. It stumbled backward long enough for the urn to fall to the ground. Rich kicked it through one of the spaces in the railing, sending it to the first floor.

"Oops," he said to the creature defiantly.

The creature turned its head and watched as the urn cracked on the tile by the fireplace. Caleb ran over to it and grabbed one of the logs from the holder. He wasted no time raising it above his head and smashing the shit out of what was left of the whale-bone urn.

The creature emitted a roar of fury and turned to Rich, but Rich was already running down the stairs. It jumped over the rail and landed on his back. Rich screamed in a way that Caleb had never heard his big brother scream. Caleb stormed the beast and pierced its eyeball with the poker, withdrawing it just as fast. The creature released Rich from its clutches and stumbled backward against the front door with its hand on its wound.

"Out the back," Rich said and led the way.

They darted through the kitchen, unlocked the back door, and sprinted out into the fenced in, frozen backyard. A seething growl came from inside the house, and then something moved on the other side of the chain link fence.

Moose. Two of them, and they were big.

They turned their heads and curiously looked at the commotion coming from Rich's house. The creature kicked open the back door. Black bile was oozing out of the hole where its eye used to be. In the moonlight, Caleb could see the dark veins through its nearly translucent skin pumping vile life into a heart of pure evil.

Caleb thought about the trapper. A plan formed in his head, but he didn't have time to consider how stupid it was with that creature now stumbling toward them and their only weapon being a fire poker. Caleb looked at Rich.

"He wants me. I'm the bait," he said, putting a hand on his older brother's shoulder. "Trust me."

Caleb hurdled the fence and landed between the two gargantuan moose. He remembered being told that they won't mess with you if you don't mess with them, and he hoped the inverse of that was true. One of the moose grunted. Caleb reared back and slapped the moose as hard as he could right across its snout. He screamed in its face and could see the wild swirling in its eyes. The other one grunted behind him, seemingly getting just as pissed.

Caleb took off, running parallel with the fence. He saw the creature out of the corner of his eye running across Rich's backyard, obviously not interested in Rich right now. Its wings expanded, and that's when Caleb knew to stop.

He stood tall and backed up against a massive tree. The ground under his feet vibrated from the two incoming moose. He watched as the half-blind, white vampire from a bygone era flapped its wings once more to get that perfect form to spear him like he had Garcia at the gate. He heard the angry grunts of the moose about to trample him.

And then he pivoted to the other side of the tree. Something on the other side rocked the tree. He heard the trample of the moose and the wail of the creature. Had it worked? Had his crazy plan based on an even crazier plan from years ago actually worked?

He squatted down with his back to the tree and listened to whatever rumble was happening on the other side. The creature growled and hissed. A moose let out a low moan. Something heavy collapsed. He listened to gurgled breaths, and then all was quiet.

"Caleb?" Rich called from the backyard. "Caleb, please tell me you're OK."

Caleb heard Rich climb the chain link fence. He stood up and stepped out from behind the tree.

"I'm OK," he said and then turned around to see what the hell actually happened.

The creature got pinned to the tree by several moose antlers, one of which burrowed straight into its black heart. Both moose were dead. One had a broken neck, and it lay flat on the ground. The one that killed the creature had a hollowed throat; one of the creatures clawed hands still gripped a handful of viscera.

Rich approached the scene and put his arm around his younger brother.

"You did it," he said with feigned breaths.

Now that the adrenaline started to wear off, Caleb began to shiver.

"I can't believe you stabbed that fuckin' thing's eye like that," Rich said.

Caleb chuckled, but it hurt.

"You're like a hunter *and* a trapper. Even though I wanna go kick that old man in his dick right now for giving you that, I think he gave it to the right person."

Caleb looked at him and smiled. He never got tired of his brother's approval.

"Can we go inside now?" he asked.

Rich chuckled.

"Yeah, but remember, I promised you a light show," he said.

Caleb looked at him quizzically.

"Trust me," he said. "We're gonna watch this one from the roof."

**

It was moments from sunrise. Caleb and Rich lay on the roof, bundled up in warm clothes, trying to be as incognito as possible. Before they had come up here, Rich had gotten Caleb's phone and called the military police and reported hearing a disturbance on their street. He told Caleb that someone needed to go get Timmy's two little girls out of that house, and then the two of them went up to the roof.

For the last few hours, they had been listening to sirens and more sirens as the base caught wind of the slaughter not just next door, but the massacre of people at the scenic overlook. Caleb had asked him how they were going to explain what happened, and Rich had assured him that there were cameras all over the base. They wouldn't be in any trouble. And he insisted on going to watch the light show, even though Caleb still didn't know what he meant by that.

Now, as the first rays of sunlight crested the mountains and began to coat the back yard, Caleb realized what his brother had been talking about. The vampire, still pinned to the tree by the moose carcass, started to sizzle and pop like bacon at first, and then it quickly became engulfed in blinding white flames that somehow produced red smoke. It only lasted about thirty seconds, but Caleb thoroughly enjoyed it. All that remained was a pile of ash melting into the snow.

"Well, that was one hell of a light show," Caleb said, turning to Rich.

When he looked at his brother, his heart skipped a beat.

Rich had pale skin, and his eyes had taken on a milky hue. Even his face looked skinnier, gaunt, as if his bones were elongating.

"Rich, what's happening?" he asked, not wanting to hear the answer.

Rich showed him his bite on his forearm.

"That vampire bastard got me when we were wrestling inside."

"We gotta get you to a doctor or something. Maybe they can stop it. I bet that old trapper would know what to do!"

Rich shook his head.

"It's too late for me, little bro. I'm already hungry and keep thinking these bad thoughts."

Tears formed in Caleb's eyes as he listened to Rich keep talking.

"I figure I have two choices right now. I can go hide in my basement, away from the world, wait until night, and see what happens. My guess is that I would probably survive. No, I know I could. But at what cost? I'd be feasting on the blood of others, ruining lives, causing chaos... stuck in an endless cycle of darkness."

For reasons Caleb wouldn't consciously admit, he could relate.

Rich continued.

"I don't want that. No..." he said as he rolled over on his back and folded his hands behind his head so that he looked straight into the sky, "I think I'll choose the light."

"Rich, please don't do this," Caleb sobbed. "Come inside."

"Shh, baby brother. We're at the beach right now. Can you hear it? Lie down with me, please," he said as he closed his eyes.

Caleb looked at his brother and wiped the tears from his face.

"OK," he said and leaned back.

He closed his eyes and did his best not to cry. He focused on his breathing, and then he focused on his brother's breathing and how it started to change.

As he began to hear the simmering sounds, and that burning smell crept in, he focused even harder, way back to life before all this, back to when they were kids and bad things didn't happen in the world. It was hard, but he did it.

And then he was at the beach with his big brother, lying on the sand, listening to sea gulls and crashing waves. He thought about the past and his future. He thought about the Northern Lights, the universe, and his place in it. He focused on the light, and the sun got a little brighter.

The End

Printed in Great Britain
by Amazon